The Land of the Free

A Novel

Patricia Milano

Booklocker.com, Inc.
2008

Dedicated to the Men and Women
Of the Greatest Generation

To My Friend
Beverly —
Enjoy
Patricia Milano

I know that freedom can only be given,
And is the gift to the giver
From the one who receives
- Wendell Berry

PROLOGUE

Mr. Kolinski came out of the shop. Nick was waiting for him. "I have something to tell you."

His boss wrinkled his forehead. "Been thinkin' you got somethin' on your mind."

"You're right. I've been thinking a lot about the attack on Pearl Harbor so today I enlisted in the Marine Corp."

Mr. Kolinski looked forlorn but a hint of pride came across his face. "I hate to see you go but I understand. I'd do the same if I were your age but I want you to know the job will be here waitin' for you when you get back."

All across the country young men like Dominic Romano were enlisting. The attack by the Japanese on their own shores had brought the war into their own domain. The war in Europe had seemed far away but now it was as though a thief had broken into their home in the middle of the night and destroyed it.

The women went to work in defense jobs and filled in any place they were needed so their men could go off to war.

Very few of these young people realized how this war would change their lives forever.

Nick had broken out of the coal-mining rut that had ruined his father's health and emotional well-being. He had dreams of college and an education that would enable him to accomplish goals that few sons of immigrants had ever dreamed. The problem was that his mother had no income and lived on a small pittance paid by the coal miners union. And so he put his scholarship in a drawer and migrated to the city to make a living any way he could to support his mother and sister. It was not a dream job but it was respectable and paid enough that he could live and still send his mother what was left so that she might also be able to put food on the table and his sister could have decent clothes for school.

The United States Government paid an allotment of a few dollars a month to the dependants of any soldier serving in the armed forces. This provided a measure of comfort for the soldiers like Nick who supported their families.

The sad thing was that Japanese Americans even those born in the United States of America were rounded up, stripped of their possessions and sent to internment camps not unlike the concentration camps in Europe minus the ovens. Paranoia was everywhere and like the witch- hunts of old was based on nothing but fear.

When the war was finally over, these men and women who have now been labeled the greatest generation went on with their life. This is the story of these men and the woman who loved them.

Land of the Free

A Novel

Patricia Milano

Colorado, 1941
Chapter I

Dominic walked slowly and deliberately as though to his execution and saw his father's face in every step. He trudged on toward the entrance of the mine. It was early morning and dawn had not yet broken through the heavy clouds that obscured the moon and stars. His thoughts were as dismal as the morning.

When he was in high school he had sworn that he would never enter, much less work in the coal mine that had killed his father's spirit and sent him on a path of destruction from which he never recovered.

"Hello Nick, how's your first week on the job?" the voice came out of the darkness and Dominic made out his old schoolmate. Hank had dropped out of school in tenth grade and was already an old hand at the mine.

"Okay, I guess."

"I never thought you'd work here, gettin' that scholarship and all."

"Mom needs the money and this is the only place in town that pays a man's wage."

"Yeah, thanks to the unions the pay's a damn sight bettern' it was when our fathers' worked here."

They came to the entrance and the elevator that took them down was filled with men that had been working here all their lives. Some were sons of father's who had worked the mines before them. Hank already had the gray pallor and hacking cough of a coal miner. Dominic knew that he could not do this. Tonight he would pick up his first paycheck and explain to his mother that he would have to go away. She would be sad but he knew she would not try to stop him. His scholarship lay at home in the bureau drawer where it would stay until he made enough money that his mother could live comfortably and his little sister would be able to go to school with decent clothes and shoes. His mother worked hard at her sewing but it was not enough to pay the bills. She had sacrificed long enough so he could graduate and now it was his turn to help her. When his father died, Dominic had vowed to be the man of the house but so far he was unable to keep that vow as far as finances were concerned.

All these things were still on Dominic's mind when they stopped work for lunch. All the men brought their lunch in metal buckets like their fathers before them and as they ate they talked about their wives and children and their everyday lives.

Suddenly there was a low rumbling sound and without provocation a section of the mine began to crumble and rain its black dusty coal down on the men. They scurried quickly to the far end of the tunnel and yelled at the men above. It was not a major cave-in but could be the beginning of one. Dominic was caught off guard and one of his legs caught the brunt of a large piece of the coal as it fell. Hank turned and came back and began to dig the piece of coal from the fine debris that covered Nick's leg. He worked furiously until he could see the leg that was bleeding through the material of his pants.

"Come on, let's get out of here before another stud gives way." He yanked Dominic's arm, put his other arm around him and dragged him toward the elevator that was already filled with men. The siren wailed and the elevator lifted its burden to the opening above. The men dusted themselves off, glad that it was no worse and then noticed that Hank had propped Domimic up against the side of the building.

"Somebody call Doc." Hank yelled as he tore Dominic's pant leg to get a look at the wound. The foreman came to his aid.

"Doc's on his way. We'll get you fixed up".

2

The other men glanced at him but no one seemed too concerned. Dominic could see the black coal dust mingled with the blood. It hurt like hell, but to the others it probably looked like nothing. It was his own fault for not moving faster.

"Thanks, Hank." Dominic said his voice still shaky.

"Don't worry, you'll be all right. Here comes Doc now."

Dominic wondered if this was the same Doctor that had been here when his father was hurt in a big cave-in. He looked old enough and walked slowly, his black bag swinging beside him. He knelt down and examined the wound, washed it with antiseptic, and covered it with gauze.

"Can you walk?" He asked. "I got my car here and I'll take you to the office where I can do a better job."

"No thanks, I'm okay. I've got to pick up my paycheck."

"Well, just be sure you keep it clean, so's it don't get infected. If it does you'll have trouble."

"I will, thanks." Dominic limped away toward the payroll office. A crazy thought came to him as he remembered his mother telling him that half the men in town limped because the doctor always scraped the bone in their leg when they were in a cave-in so the coal dust couldn't infect them. It had been a close call but he knew that he would never again enter that mine.

Dominic tried to sneak past his mother but as always she seemed to have eyes in the back of her head.

"What happened?" She asked without turning away from her sewing machine. "I heard the siren but it wasn't the long one that tells you it's really bad."

"I didn't know there was a difference. It was just a small cave-in where a stud came down. Nobody was hurt."

"So why is your pant leg hanging loose with blood on it?" Her voice was dry as she turned to face him.

Nick grinned at her. "So a piece of coal hit my leg. Hey Ma, it was nothing this time." He handed her the paycheck. "That's not to say it couldn't be worse next time."

"I know." She said glancing at the check. "I told you not to do this. We'll get by."

Nick put his hand on her shoulder and lifted her chin so he could look her straight in the eye before saying what he had practiced in his mind. "Ma, I'm going to Denver and find a job. I'll send you all the money I can but I've got to do this."

His mother put her hand over his and squeezed his fingers. "What about school?"

"It will have to wait."

His mother nodded and it was settled. On Monday morning he would take the bus to Denver and look for a job.

Chapter II

Dominic sat on a bench in the park across from the Capitol. He could see the mountain range in the distance. High peaks were tinged with snow and the lower range with blue and purple hues. He was tired and discouraged but the sight of the gold dome of the huge building that was the capitol of Colorado lifted his spirits. He remembered coming here with his mother when she became a citizen and felt lucky and privileged that he had been born a citizen of this fine country. He knew he had set his sights high looking for work as a clerk when he had so little experience but he would be willing to do anything that paid a decent wage.

He ate the sandwich his mother had sent with him of thick bread with cold sausage and peppers and saw a service station on the corner of the street east of the capitol building. Pumping gas was not what he had envisioned doing but he decided that "beggars can't be choosers" as his mother often said, and walked across the street. A man in coveralls had just finished waiting on a customer whowas pulling away.

"Hello!" Nick called. He had come to the city dressed in his best and only suit. His shirt was starched and shone a brilliant white against his dark jacket and tie. His hair was dark brown tinged with copper and waved back from his brow. He was a fine looking young man and was smiling as he came up to the man.

The man nodded. "What can I do for you?"

"I was wondering if you knew if there were any jobs around."

The man looked him up and down and said, "It's not what you're lookin' for I guess, but I could sure use someone around here to pump gas so I don't have to stop what I'm doin' in the garage to come out every time a car pulls in."

In a short time, Nick and the man whose name was Joe Kolinski had negotiated a deal and Nick had a job. The only thing still pending was to find a place to stay. His suitcase was in a locker at the bus station and contained only underwear and socks and an extra shirt. Mr. Kolinski had a solution for everything. There was a rooming house down the block and he had uniforms for the man up front including a sharp cap with the gas company's logo and a shiny black brim. The Chinese laundry across the street furnished three clean uniforms a week for a small sum that he would deduct from Nick's pay.

"So can you start in the morning?" Mr. Kolinski asked.

"Sure thing, sir." Nick liked this man. His hair was streaked with gray and his eyes had worry wrinkles that ran down his cheeks. His shoulders were broad and a red rag hung from the pocket of his dirty coveralls.

"Good, I'm sure the rooming house'll do. The landlady, Mrs. O'Grady, is an Irish widow and I hear tell she makes a tasty stew." His voice sounded relieved that everything appeared to be settled and he could get back to work

Nick found the rooming house with no trouble. It sat on a side street that had been residential at one time but now most of the other houses had been turned into small businesses. It looked to be three stories although the top story narrowed considerably with one small window under the peaked eave. A sign in front looked as old as the house and read simply ROOM AND BOARD. A tall woman with orange hair partially covered with a scarf answered the door.

"Do you have a room available?" Nick asked.

"Mebbe, depends on who ya' might be and your business."

Nick smiled his most charming smile. "I'm Mr. Kolinski's new attendant, Nick Romano and it was him who recommended you."

"Sure, and it's a fine man he is too. The room's in the attic, it tis' and some think it's too much climbin' those stairs, but for a young man like yourself it should be a snap."

Nick's smile widened. "Sounds fine to me ma'am."

"Then come along" she said leading the way. "You'll be more private up here for sure."

The room contained a single bed with a nightstand and a rocking chair of maple wood with a cushion of dark green wool. A commode in the corner had an old- fashioned pitcher and basin. A white towel and facecloth hung neatly beside them. Nick glanced around noting there was no bathroom. She seemed to read his mind.

"The bathroom's on the floor below, but I'll bring you a kettle of hot water every morning so you can spruce up."

"How many share the bathroom?"

"Just one woman who sleeps late and a bread delivery man who leaves real early in the morning. There's a sign to put up if it's occupied." Mrs. O'Grady appeared nonchalant "I have hot coffee in the morning for who wants it and supper at six in the evening. Anything else is up to you."

"I'll take it." Nick knew this was all he could afford and he was lucky to get it.

Nick lay on the bed with his arms behind his head. It was Sunday and he had gone to Mass at the big cathedral on Colfax Avenue. It was the largest church he had ever seen and when he walked down the aisle he felt small and insignificant. The stain glass windows cast rainbow shafts across the heads of the congregation. The altar was gold and marble and the priests wore colorful garments trimmed in gold. The voices of the choir echoed in the vast arches as the statuary saints looked frozen in time.

Nick thought of his mother kneeling in the plain church of his childhood and felt a wave of home- sickness for her and his sister. Lord knew his life had been hard as a boy. He'd worked the sugar beets in the summer and walked eight miles to school in the winter, but he always had good food, a place to sleep and love of family. It was only thirty miles home, but the price of the bus would only take away from the money he could send to his mother. He had envisioned a better job, but times were hard and he knew he was lucky to have found a decent place to work.

There were rumblings of the United States joining England and their allies in the fight against Hitler. Many of the young men had already joined and as much as he was tempted, Nick felt that first and foremost he must help his mother. He had been out of school since June and had not accomplished much other than to get away from the mine.

Nick had been at the station for over six months and it had been a good arrangement. He worked long hours so Mr. Kolinski could take in more mechanical work that in turn made him more money so he could afford to pay Nick. Mr. Kolinski had a daughter who was married and lived in California and a wife who kept his books and cooked his meals but he had always longed for a son and Nick was rapidly fulfilling that dream. He had even told Nick that if he continued to work for him that someday he would make him a partner.

Nick was a hard worker, the customers liked him and he was smart. He kept meticulous records and could count the cash drawer in half the time it took Mr. Kolinski.

One day in early December all of that changed. Nick picked up the newspaper on his way to the station. He was shocked to see the headlines, JAPS ATTACK PEARL HARBOR. Graphic pictures of the desolation showed hundreds of navy men, black and burned floating in the harbor as their ships were destroyed. Nick felt an outrage he had never felt before. How dare they do that to this wonderful country? He had been brought up to revere this country as a haven and land of opportunity. His mother had instilled that in him and his two sisters from her own experience. She and his father had come from Italy to this country to be free. It had not discouraged her that life had not been perfect.

As the days went by Nick, like many young men, felt he had to join in the service. He went to the recruitment office and looked at the various branches. He knew there was a good chance that he would be drafted but he decided that he did not want to wait for that to decide his fate.

The Marine poster was the most vivid and exciting. Nick stood staring, trying to imagine himself as resplendent in that uniform as the handsome young man in the poster. He knew that the reputation of the Marines was one of dedication and heroic deeds and doubted that this picture was an accurate portrayal of the average fighting Marine. The poster stirred his soul and he threw back his shoulders and lifted his chin.

Nick had been sending his mother most of his hard earned salary. He kept only the necessary money for rent and food. Would he still be able to do that as well? His years of poverty had made him cautious, but his patriotism and pride overruled his doubts and he marched through the door.

"Hi, young man. How are you this morning?" The sergeant was in a brown uniform and looked nothing like the man in the poster.

"Fine, Sir. I wanted to ask some questions about enlisting."

"You've come to the right place, my man. Pull up a chair and we'll go over some of the hi-lights of a career in the finest branch of the service."

When Nick came out of the recruiting station he had signed the papers for his enlistment and was to report for duty in two weeks. The sergeant had assured him that he was entitled to an allotment that would be paid each month to his next of kin, namely his mother. They also had an insurance policy in case of his death that would be paid to his mother. These two things greatly relieved the burden that Nick felt his absence would cause. The next thing was to break the news to his boss.

"Where've been Nick?" Mr. Kolinski was waiting impatiently. "You're late. Guess I'm gonna have to get you one of them there watches."

"Sorry," Nick checked the cash drawer just as the first car of the day pulled in.

The day went by quickly and at six o'clock, Mr.Kolinski came out of the shop. Nick was waiting for him. "I have something I have to tell you," he began. Mr. Kolinski wrinkled his forehead.

"Been thinkin' you got somethin' on your mind. You been actin' kind of funny lately."

" You're right, I've been thinking a lot about the attack on Pearl Harbor and that I should be doing something so I enlisted in the Marine Corp today."

Mr. Kolinski looked forlorn but a hint of pride also came across his face. He shook his head. "I hate to see you go, boy, but I understand. I'd be the same if I was your age."

"Thanks," Nick looked relieved. "I've got two weeks. Maybe we can find somebody."

Mr. Kolinski shrugged, "Did it by myself before. Just want ya to know, ther'll always be a job here for you when you get back."

"Thanks." The two men shook hands.

The station was closed on Sunday due to the fact that all the government offices in the area were closed and partly due to

Mr. Kolinski's observance of the Sabbath. It was his only day of rest and he felt it was worth it.

Dominic took the bus to Louisville without giving his mother any advance notice. He knew her routine as well as he knew the sun would rise each morning. She went to Mass daily, but Sunday was special and she went with the idea that she would see many friends and stop and chat. She might even invite someone to dinner if the fancy struck her. Anna would be singing in the choir and occasionally had a solo. She had the voice of an angel, the people said, and Dominic was proud of his young sister.

Dominic arrived just as his mother was putting dinner on the table and he could smell the tomato sauce and garlic and spices as he neared the door. Mrs. O' Grady's stew paled by comparison.

"Nicky!" Anna screamed seeing him first. She flung herself at him and he picked her up, whirling her around.

"Mama!" Nick picked her up as he had Anna and at her laughing squeals set her down.

"Why didn't you tell us you were coming?" Mama was quickly adding another place to the table. "I would have invited your aunt and uncle."

" I'd rather it was just us, Mama."

"Is something wrong? You lost your job eh?"

Nick shook his head, "Let's eat, it looks so good. Then we'll talk."

Mama said grace and piled Nick's plate with chicken and pasta and vegetables. The bread was warm and fragrant and Nick ate until he was sure he would burst. Mama brought out some delicate cookies and poured a cup of hot coffee laced with whiskey.

"Now, tell me what's troubling you."

There was only one way to say it and Nick told her as he had Mr. Kolinski that he felt an obligation to his country and wanted to serve.

"It is right." Mama looked him straight in the eye her own eyes filled with tears. "God will be with you."

"You will get a check from the government every month, Mama. It won't be much but it will help."

"I am grateful but mainly I hope you will serve honorably and safely and come home to us soon."

As he left to catch the bus back to Denver, Dominic felt such peace in his mother's love he knew in his heart that he would come back. It would be a great adventure. He was young and strong and ready for anything. The stories of the Marines being the toughest branch of the service only made Nick more determined than ever.

New Years Eve that brought in 1942 meant nothing to Nick although he could hear the celebrations in the city through the walls of the rooming house. He had no money to spend and his friends were all back in Louisville. He couldn't help feeling a little lonely and was pleased when Mr. Kolinski invited him to his home the next day for the holiday dinner. Nick knew this would be his last home cooked meal in a long time.

Mrs. Kolinski proved to be a pleasant lady of massive proportions and a much better cook than his landlady. The pork roast, mashed potatoes, gravy and biscuits were topped off with a delicious apple pie. Nick enjoyed their company and was feeling much less lonely. This was a good way to start the New Year and he was sure 1942 would be full of adventure.

The day to report for duty had arrived and Nick was surprised to see how many young men were being sworn in. As an avid reader, Nick knew that the whole country had risen to the occasion when the Japanese attacked Pearl Harbor. It was deeply personal, not unlike a burglar attacking your own home in the middle of the night. Women were rallying to the cause as well, working long hours in the defense plants, selling war bonds and growing their own food.

After standing in long lines and passing the physical Nick was issued a uniform and headed for the barber. The clippers buzzed and his curls fell in a heap on the floor. He rubbed his head gingerly wondering if he looked like a typical recruit. He was anxious to know where he was going and what he would be doing. A tall lanky kid named James Conelly had been close behind Nick through all the lines and into the barbershop. He rubbed his head too.

"Feels good don't it?" He was watching as Nick placed his cap at a rakish angle.

" Cool, anyhow." Nick replied.

When everyone had been processed they were loaded into large open trucks with benches on both sides. The road they took was hot, dusty and rough. James sat quietly next to Dominic with a look of confusion.

"Where ya' think we're headin?"

"I heard some of the guys talking and they said we're going to boot camp right here in Colorado."

James wrinkled his forehead, "Damn, I thought we'd go on a train. I ain't never been on a train."

"Boot camp's only thirty days. We're sure to be sent someplace after that."

They arrived at camp, tired, dusty and disgruntled and as they piled out of the trucks, Nick could not see the slightest resemblance to the beautiful state of Colorado. There were no mountains to be seen, only acres of brown dirt with scruffy bushes and gulches spread across the plains. In the distance massive old cottonwoods bent their thick branches low to the ground nearly touching the dirt. There must be a stream nearby to nurture those trees, Nick thought as he scanned the terrain. Quonset huts of gray metal were set in long rows facing each other, the only structures in this barren place. A sign on the Quonset hut nearest the trucks read MESS HALL and all eyes turned toward it hopefully since they had not eaten since breakfast.

"Atten-shun!" the sergeant shouted and the men shuffled into place and stood at attention. "You have all been issued a duffel bag containing your clothes and necessary items. File to your quarters, drop your bag at the end of your bed and return to line up for chow. You will be issued your rifle as you return to quarters. Reveille will be at 0500. You will report here on the field at 0530 for calisthenics, breakfast is at 0600. You will then be briefed on your schedule of the day. Dismissed!"

The men filed into their quarters as they were told and then headed back to the Mess Hall. James stuck close to Nick looking like a frightened kindergartner on his first day at school. Nick was not all that self-assured himself but would have died before showing it.

The days began to take on a routine and Nick had to admit he had learned a lot. He could now dismantle and assemble his rifle in record time, hike relentless distances with a full pack and go all day with only one small canteen of water and a can of C-rations. At first he had been so sore after hiking or climbing obstacles that he had thought he would surely die in his sleep, but he always woke up and did it all over again. Just when he thought he was getting used to hiking they double-timed it. Hand grenade and gas mask practice was realistic to say the least. His hands and feet were covered with blisters and stung like hell when water touched them. He had thought mining was hard but this was worse.

The boot camp training was painfully tough. To the drill instructors you were an object of humiliation. They shouted in your face, spittle spewing from their mouth, their foul breath causing you to gag. Could you prove to them that you were not just a sniveling boy but a man of stamina?

The drill instructor stood before them. His ebony face screwed into a snarl. His neck, thick as a bulls, his massive arms grasped his rifle. A thick stick hung from his belt. His voice was a raspy scream.

" I'm hear to teach you not only to fight for your country but for your life!"

He believed it and nothing would deter him from his mission.

The platoon was subject to a barrage of lectures on everything from weapons to venereal disease and if you were caught nodding off during lectures you were disciplined. Penalties for any type of failures were severely administered.

One day as they stood in line Nick stared in horror as the drill instructor put a bucket over James's head and made him yell at the top of his lungs, "I am a shit head" one hundred times.

Nick's face reddened in humiliation for his friend and he noticed that James's fly was open. The punishment seemed extreme but was typical of the drill instructor's code.

Another of their group called his rifle a "gun" and for punishment had to walk up and down in front of them holding a rifle in his right hand, his left hand holding his genitals while reciting, "This is my rifle, this is my gun. One is for work, the other's for fun!"

This type of punishment was so degrading that many of the men became bullies themselves to offset the shame they felt, while others turned silent and moody.

Nick hated the humiliation but tried to understand the basic reality that they had all led a comparatively soft life and if they were to survive in this terrible war they needed to be tough.

Nick wrote to his mother every Sunday no matter how tired he was and gave her no impression what it was really like. He hoped the government would be true to their word and she would get her allotment check every month.

The time had finally come that they had completed the program and were now "full fledged" Marines. They were to receive their assignments, get seven days leave and report to their assigned stations. At last the officers seemed almost human and the last night they had a party with beer for those who wanted it and Pepsi for those who didn't. The cooks made large piazzas and were actually jovial as they handed out the treat. Many of those who had the most difficult time now seemed the proudest of their accomplishment.

In the morning the trucks were lined up to take them back to the city and they were handed a paycheck and their assignment. They looked at their assignments first. Many were headed for bases in California where they would no doubt be shipped to the South Pacific. Nick was shocked to read of his assignment to a radio communications school in Michigan. This was not what he had in mind. He had always imagined that he would go to the South Pacific. He tried to hide his disappointment amid the shouts of his cohorts and then he saw James looking lost and puzzled. They had become good friends during the month of grueling hardships and he had learned to like the shy young man who had lived his life on a farm in southern Colorado raising lettuce and beans and other food exports. His mother and father and three sisters had hated losing him at a time when the country needed the food products even more, but like all Americans they wanted to give to their country and if it meant their only son then so be it.

James came to Nick looking sad, "I don't understand it. I'm assigned to radio communications school and Sarge says it's a big honor but I wanted to go fight the Japs."

Nick slapped him on the back. "Hey, guy, that's my assignment too so we'll be together."

A broad smile spread across James long face and tears glazed his eyes. "I'm so glad I'll be with you. Damn, I was really scared!" He grabbed Nick in a bear hug then stepped back embarrassed.

"Well, there's just one thing." Nick was smiling too. "What in the hell are we going to do in Michigan?"

Chapter III
Michigan 1941

Josie unlaced her ice skates, tied them together and slung them over her shoulder. The clubhouse was noisy with talk and laughter and smelled of wet mittens and wood burning in the large stone fireplace. Occasionally some one backed up too close to the fire and the odor of scorched wool filled the air. It was Saturday night and Josie and her friends had been at the Winter Sports Park since early afternoon. Josie loved the camaraderie in the clubhouse after a day of skating and tobogganing. She sat with a hotdog and cocoa brimming with marshmallows, dreading going back to the house. It would be empty except for her grandfather hunched close to the coal stove.

"So long Ruthie. See you in church." Josie drained her cup.

"Okay, Josie. Want us to come and pick you up?"

"No, my mother will bring me if she doesn't have to work." Josie wrapped her scarf around her neck and left. A full moon smiled down on the white snow turning it to sparkling silver. Josie climbed the hill through the forest. In 1941 it was not presumed dangerous to go home alone. At the top of the hill, she sat on the path melted just enough during the day to be glazed with ice when the sun went down. She looked up at the tall pines and the bare branches of the aspen making a lacey pattern across the moon and smiled. She knew what she was about to do was hard on her pants. *Okay she whispered, taking a deep breath. I can do this!* She gave herself a push. The icy path twisted and turned through the snow-laden trees as she went flying down the hill and landed in a pile of snow. She laughed as she brushed herself off and walked the few remaining yards to the back door.

"Hi Grampa, it's not too cold tonight for December."

"Cold enough. I've stoked the fire good though to hold 'til morning."

"Is Mom home yet?"

"No, probably had to work. You hungry?"

" I had a hotdog at the park."

Josie headed up the stairs and Grampa shuffled into the only downstairs bedroom.

Sometime later Josie heard her mother come upstairs and smelled the smoke from her cigarette as she prepared for bed. Mother never smoked downstairs. Her father did not approve of women smoking and it *was* his house.

Josie's alarm sounded. She covered her head and burrowed deeper in the blankets. The heat from the stove never reached upstairs and it was freezing. She finally reached out, turned off the alarm, and dressed hurriedly. She peeked into her mother's room but she was still sleeping soundly. Josie went downstairs to the makeshift bathroom, then grabbing her coat from the hook and pulling on her boots, went out into the frosty daylight to walk the few miles to church.

Her stomach growled and she hoped that the Ladies Guild would serve doughnuts after the service.

Ruthie met her in the vestibule. "You look frozen. You walked didn't you?"

"Yeah, my Mom looked like she was really tired, so I didn't wake her."

"We're going out for breakfast and my Dad said you can come, okay?"

Josie smiled shyly. "Wow, that would be great."

As Mr. Baumberg and the girls entered the restaurant, it seemed strangely quiet. The radio that usually played soft music for the patrons was tuned to President Roosevelt's voice with his distinguished eastern accent.

Every one was listening. *Dec.7th , 1941- a date which will live in infamy- the United States of America was suddenly and deliberately attacked by naval and air forces of the Empire of Japan.*

Josie looked about her at the faces listening so intently and saw fear, disbelief and even anger. Everyone had stopped eating. Coffee sat cooling in the cups and food lay untouched on their plates.

President Roosevelt continued, *I will ask that Congress declare that since the unprovoked and dastardly attack by Japan on Sunday, December 7, a state of war has existed between the United States and the Japanese empire.*

A man stood up and shouted. "Those bastards!"

The woman seated with him pulled him back into his chair. Others began to talk among themselves. The proprietor quickly turned off the radio and motioned them to a table. Josie shivered as a chill came over her and though she had little idea of what it all meant, somehow she knew that nothing would ever be quite the same again.

Chapter IV

Josephine Ann Mofford was the only child of divorced parents that in 1941 was either a show of high sophistication or an object of pity by the straight and narrow Methodists of this small Michigan town. Unfortunately, Josies's mother fell into the latter category. She had married a city man who walked out one day to find a job in Detroit and never came back.

It was a bitter blow to her mother's pride, but fortunately Josie's grandfather lived alone in the large old house that had been her mother's girlhood home. Josie and her mother moved in on the pretense of caring for the aging man.

It was a lonely life for a teenage girl but Josie found solace in books. She read everything from the classics to the" best sellers." The most wonderful one at the moment was the novel "Gone with the Wind". Josie *was* Scarlet and reveled in the exciting places and people of the romantic world she read about. She was a pretty girl with hair the color of honey and eyes as blue as the great lake that lapped against the shores of their town.

The winter passed quickly for Josie. It was her senior year of high school and added to her studies was her appointment as editor of the yearbook. It was an awesome responsibility and she dug in as though her life depended on it. She gathered her staff from the top students of Journalism and Art and convinced them to work as hard as she did.

Many of the young men of the class of '42 had enlisted following the declaration of war and would be leaving for their various assignments the day after graduation. They were impatient and school was boring compared to the excitement of "getting into the action."

"Come on Josie, go to the party with me." John held the door of her locker open. "You work on that darn book every night."

"If I don't work on that "darn book", you won't have a yearbook to look at when you're in the Army."

"Do you think I'll have time to be looking at pictures?" John stood aside as Josie closed her locker. "I'll be fightin' those Japs. Come on, please. We don't have much time left."

"Okay, pick me up at seven."

"Yeah!" John pumped his fist in the air. "See you then."

Josie sighed. *Why were the guys so anxious to go off and get killed?* Josie read the reports in the paper and knew that the war was not going well. Men were getting killed and captured by the thousands. *Boys never think things through. To them it's all a big game.*

Josie and John were sitting in her driveway in his '36 Ford coupe. The party had been wild and noisy. The girls were the so-called "in" crowd and the boys were the football and basketball jocks. Josie was not usually invited since she was not a cheerleader but John was the popular captain of the basketball team and could bring anyone he pleased. Someone had brought beer that the guys drank with gusto. They seemed to reason that if they were old enough to go to war they were old enough to drink. There had been plenty of cigarettes too, and the odor of beer and cigarettes had followed them into the car.

"You look so pretty tonight." John's voice slurred and was followed by a hiccup.

Josie tried to move closer to the door as John bent his tall frame to kiss her. One hand slid up under her dress.

"No, John." Josie pushed him away. "You smell like beer and I've got to go in."

"Come on, don't be like that. I might be dead in a few months."

"You'll be dead before that if you don't let me out of here." Josie opened the door and nearly fell out. She slammed it shut and ran up the walk to the back door.

Before she reached the steps, the door opened and there stood her grandfather in a flannel nightshirt, his balding head shining under the kitchen light. "Everything all right?"

"Sure, Grampa, I'm going up to bed."

Many times she had been annoyed when her grandfather was peeking at her but tonight it made her feel safe. She heard John's car backing away and couldn't help but think that he was much too young and immature to be going off to war.

The day before graduation Josie received two surprises. Three really, if you counted the accolade she received the night before. She had been given an honorary award for her work as editor of the yearbook. It came in the form of a small scholarship to the local college. Josie was thrilled. She had never dreamed that she would be able to go to school since they had no money and she would be expected to work and earn her keep as soon as possible. The second surprise was a phone call from her favorite person in the whole world, Aunt Leah. She and Uncle Dan were coming for her graduation.

Still riding high on last night's achievement and Aunt Leah's phone call, Josie was flabbergasted to see a large black car pull into the driveway. A portly man with wavy gray hair came up the path and she recognized the father she had not seen in two years.

"Hello Josephine," he called as she stepped outside.

"Hi Dad." She went toward his outstretched arms and they kissed awkwardly.

"You've grown into a beautiful young lady."

"Yeah, well, " Josie blushed then shrugged.

"I got your invitation and couldn't believe you are already graduating. We were on our way up north for the summer so I thought we'd stop by." Josie saw a woman with silver hair and sparkling earrings sitting in the car.

" Come meet my wife, Emily"

"Bring her and come in, " Josie said remembering her manners.

"We can't stay. I just wanted to drop off this little gift and we'll be on our way."

Her father handed her a small package wrapped in gold paper and took her arm and led her to the car.

"Emily, this is Josephine."

The woman extended her hand through the window, " It's a pleasure my dear."

And to her husband she said, "Come on, let's get on the road or we'll be late for the dinner party."

Josie's father was already climbing in to the drivers seat. "It was nice to see you. Be sure and write."

He started the car and was gone. Josie waved as the rear of the car disappeared.

Josie felt tears stinging her eyes. Why did she have such weird parents? Last night no one had been there when the scholarship was awarded and probably no one would come to her graduation. Josie laid the package on the table. No matter what it was, it couldn't be as good as having a mom and dad come to graduation together.

She went back into the house with a heavy heart. John would be by shortly to take her to dinner and yet another dumb party. She knew she really didn't fit into his crowd but she was lonely and if he liked her and wanted her with him, she had decided she'd go anyway.

She took a beautiful dress from the closet. She bought it with the money she made working in one of the resort shops. They had let her have it at a really good price because they were moving to Florida for the winter and the less stock they had the better. It was a midnight blue taffeta with a full skirt and sweetheart neckline. She had planned to save it for graduation but she reasoned that she could wear it both times since her gown would cover it tomorrow. Her shiny leather pumps with slim heels made her feel like a lady. She looked in the mirror and fluffed her hair. The gold package lay on the table and she picked it up, opening it slowly. The box inside was black velvet and nestled inside was a gold watch. It was slim and trim and as she slipped it on her wrist the tiny gold words Bulova shown from its face. It's a beautiful watch she thought happily. Her friends would be surprised. She heard the horn of John's car and ran outside.

They pulled up in front of a house that was lit from top to bottom. It was large with three stories and loud music filled the air. At the door an attractive woman welcomed them. "I'm Sherrie's mother. Oh hello John. I don't believe I know your young lady."

"Hi Mrs. Longcore. This is Josie Mofford."

"Come on in. There's a buffet set up on the back patio." Mrs. Longcore said, leading them through the house.

Josie glanced at the rooms as they made their way to the patio. It reminded her of a layout in a magazine. Everything was perfect.

There was the usual crowd filling their plates and talking and laughing. Sherrie greeted John, barely glancing at Josie, "Have some food John and …Josie isn't it?"

Josie nodded. John put his arm around her and they filled their plates. John found her a seat and brought her a glass of punch.

Josie began to relax and even laughed at some of the chatter. It was about eight o'clock when Sherrie's parents came outside.

"We're on our way out" her mother said. Annie will clean up and you can dance or play games. You're adults now." She laughed and they were gone.

The party seemed to take on a more exciting tone and the music was loud and fast. As the evening wore on, couples started disappearing into different rooms or laying on the floor listening to music wrapped up in one another.

John kept Josie's glass filled with punch that tasted exceptionally good tonight. The music now was slow and couples were dancing close with eyes closed. John pressed her against him. "You are so beautiful tonight. Your eyes are the same color as your dress."

Josie smiled up at him. It felt good snuggling in his arms. They danced inside and John took her hand and led her through an open door. It was a library with books reaching from floor to ceiling, a desk and a leather couch that smelled wonderful. John closed the door and pulled her down on the couch. He caressed her face and ran his hand across her back rubbing it gently. Josie snuggled against him. She felt so relaxed and dreamy. Suddenly he had his hands under her dress, pulling down her panties and stockings. "No, John," she whispered.

"Yes, oh Josie I want you so bad. Just once before I leave. You're so sweet." He undid his belt and his pants fell to the floor. He held her close touching her gently, at first and then he was inside her with a deep hard thrust. He groaned, shuddered and sagged against her.

There were footsteps in the hall and John jumped up pulling on his pants. He motioned Josie to a door and she picked up her panties and stockings and ran. It was a small bathroom. Josie eyes filled with tears. This was not how she had dreamed it would be. It was horrible and degrading. Where was her resistance? The punch, it was spiked! How naïve and stupid could she be? She had spoiled everything. She wiped gently with a tissue and saw the blood. It's over. She had lost the virginity that she had protected and cherished for her first real love and now it would never be the same.

The next morning as they lined up for their diplomas Josie still felt the shame of last night's fiasco. John had tricked her and the disgust that she felt for him was matched only by her feeling of disgust for herself.

"Josie," she looked up to see her Aunt Leah waving and pushing her way through the crowd. "We made it! I was afraid we'd be late."

"Auntie Leah, I'm so glad to see you." Josie felt a lump in her throat. Her aunt and uncle had driven 400 miles to see her graduate. At last the happiness of the day surrounded her. They had even stopped by the house and picked up Grandpa who was smiling proudly. Josie looked for her mother but decided she had not made it. Then she saw her pushing her way through the crowd to join them.

"Sorry I'm late but I had trouble getting away."

After the festivities were over and they were back at the house Aunt Leah smiled at Josie. "I have an announcement, my dear. For your graduation gift we are taking you on a trip!"

"A trip?"

"Yes, your uncle is being transferred to New York and you are going with us to see our new apartment and go sightseeing. It's a wondrous place with the tallest buildings in the world and the statue of liberty and much more. You will love it!"

Josie hugged her aunt tightly. "I don't know what to say."

Mother and Grandpa looked as surprised as Josie. "You spoil her dreadfully." Mother said petulantly. "She has to work this summer, you know."

"We'll have her back in two weeks. We're only going to look things over. We have to come back and pack and lease our house. This is a temporary thing for the duration of the war."

Mother shrugged her shoulders and sighed. "Well I guess the decision has been made. By the way your present from me will fit right in." She handed Josie a package.

Josie took off the paper carefully. It was a pair of soft print pajamas. "Thank you Mama. I really need them."

Grampa handed her a plain white envelope. "Here." He said gruffly pressing it into her hand. "This might come in handy."

Josie took out a twenty dollar bill. "Thanks Grampa." She gave him a hug and he turned away embarrassed. They were not a demonstrative family and hugging and kissing were a rarity, but for the first time in ages Josie felt that they really did care for her and a warm feeling spread through her.

Josie looked around her at Grandfather's house. It was not a bad house at all. It was just that Josie knew her mother still felt like a girl here. She had no say so in the decoration or arrangement of furniture and they both knew that Grampa had never even removed Grandma's clothes from the bedroom where they had slept over forty years. I must be growing up Josie thought because I really understand how Mother must feel not having a home of her own. Josie had a strange feeling that when she left on the trip with her Aunt and Uncle it would be the last time she would ever live in this house.

Chapter V

Josie sat stiffly in the car that had come to pick her up at the train station. It belonged to her mother's friend, Mrs. Fryman. Not that she was really a friend but she and her husband owned the restaurant where her mother worked so as a friendly gesture she had offered to bring Josie home.

"I think it's lovely that you're going to work at the defense plant, dear. They do so need good help." Mrs. Fryman's voice was terse.

"Yes, ma'am so I've heard." Josie did not think it was lovely at all but she knew better than to voice her thoughts. She had been bitterly disappointed to receive a letter from her mother asking that she return from New York at once to go to work. She was having a wonderful time with Aunt Leah who was in New York getting the apartment ready for their move from Michigan. Aunt Leah had taken her to a beauty shop and had her hair cut and styled and they had gone to a grand live show at the Paladium, featuring Sammy Kay and his orchestra. It was called "Do you want to lead a band?" and Josie had been picked from the audience to go on stage. It was so exciting and she had led the band to the song inspired by soldiers going off to war, *"DON'T SIT UNDER THE APPLE TREE WITH ANYONE ELSE BUT ME."*

Josie did a pretty good job and won some tickets to a Broadway show and an autographed baton from Sammy Kay. It was a thrilling experience and she could hardly wait to tell Ruthie and her friends.

Aunt Leah had smiled when Josie showed her the letter. "It sounds like an order so we'd better get you on the train."

"Do I have to?' Josie asked.

"I'm afraid so. I promised your mother you'd be back in two weeks remember?"

Josie nodded. "She got me a job at the defense plant in Grand Rapids."

"It's just for the duration of the war. Then you can use your scholarship and go back to school."

Josie left the following day. Aunt Leah kissed her and promised that when the war was over she could come back.

Mrs. Fryman pulled up in front of the house and Josie hopped out. "Thanks for the ride."

Josie carried her suitcase to the door and Grandpa opened it with a smile. "We missed you." He took the suitcase and put it with two others that stood behind the door.

"Who's going away?"

Grandpa shook his head. "Didn't your mother tell you? You leave on the bus for Grand Rapids in the morning."

Josie tried to digest the events of the last few days but she had the feeling her life was already being arranged with or without her approval. She turned and went down the path toward the lake. She sat down on her favorite log and listened to the sound of water lapping against the shore. The sun was just beginning to turn the sky to orange and the fluffy white clouds were edged in pink and would soon dissolve like cotton candy. The water reflected the orange rays and shimmered and danced from the horizon to the sand at her feet. She sighed as the last rays touched her face and dried the tears that lay on her cheeks. A shadow fell as the orange ball slipped slowly into the bay and disappeared. A chill came over her and she wrapped her arms around her knees, huddling there until darkness enveloped her.

"Josephine!"

Her mother's voice cut through the air and Josie unwound to see that night had fallen. She didn't know how long she had been here but the lights sparkled across the water and her feet were wet and cold. She stood up and cupping her hands to her mouth she shouted back, "Coming! I 'm on my way."

Her voice lingered on the night air and floated to where her mother stood on the front porch. "Are you crazy out there in the dark? I fixed some supper. We need to talk."

Josie came into the circle of light from the bulb on the porch's ceiling. "Hi, I'm sorry, I didn't realize it had gotten so dark." Her mother made no move to greet her but turned and went into the house.

There was cold ham, tomatoes, lettuce, radishes and brown bread spread out on the kitchen table. A bowl of plump red strawberries and a pitcher of thick cream completed the meal. Her grandfather had already eaten, judging by his empty plate, and he had moved to his chair by the radio to listen to the news.

"I've packed your things and bought your ticket on the bus to Grand Rapids. You know I said that you needed to work. Well, they've been advertising in the paper that the defense plants need women. I'd go myself if it weren't for him." She nodded at the old man hunched in his chair. "The money is much more than anything you could make here."

"But I don't know anyone there."

"You'll get acquainted and I've made arrangements for you to room at a friend of Mrs. Fryman."

Oh God, some little old dried up Jewish widow. Josie began picking up the dishes as her thoughts leaped ahead and she was silent.

"It will be much cheaper and safer than any other place you could find. She's lived there for years and knows the neighborhood."

"So where's the job?"

"A short ride on the city bus."

"You've got it all figured out haven't you?" Josie's voice sounded hopeless and she hurried up the stairs before she said something she might regret.

The bus pulled into the station and Josie gathered her luggage. With the address of her landlady and that of the defense plant held firmly between her teeth, she sought the city bus line. She thought of the fun she and Aunt Leah had in New York and the promise of college and she wanted to scream. *How am I ever going to get out of Michigan?*

Chapter VI

It had been a long two weeks since Nick and James and six other men from their unit had come to the school in Grand Rapids to study radio communication. It was part study, part workshop and the absence of a drill instructor was heaven. Lieutenant Henry Briggs was the instructor for the study class and Sergeant Earl McKinney or Mac as the men called him took over the mechanics of the radios. Nick had never done anything mechanical and was surprised at his aptitude. The book part was easy for him and he found it fascinating. Nick had expected to go straight into combat and was not sure if he should be disappointed or relieved to have this respite.

Tonight all eight of them were headed for the Pub in town for some food, music and relaxation. Nick had always loved music. He recalled as a boy how he had cranked the phonograph and listened to the opera sitting at his father's feet. He knew he was a damn good dancer too. At the senior prom his teacher and chaperone Miss Chambry had made him dance with her and he had been proud to show off his fancy steps until she had danced him outside.

"Where did you learn to dance like that?" she panted feigning breathlessness. Nick shrugged, embarrassed and was suddenly aware that she was pressing her body against him still moving sensuously to the music. Her cheek was resting against his and her lips brushed his ear. He felt himself grow hard and then with a shudder he felt the wetness running down his leg. Her soft laugh made him panic and he had run all the way home, leaving his date Mary to go home with friends.

"Hey Nick, come on, let's go."

Nick came out of his reverie. It had been a long time since he had danced or kissed a girl. Maybe he'd get lucky tonight.

Josie was not thrilled with her room at Mrs. Goldmans. It was small and smelled like old quilts stored in the attic. Josie swore that Mrs. Goldman went through her things trying to find something she could gossip about or report to Mrs. Fryman. The supper that came with her room was served in the kitchen on a table covered with faded oilcloth. The food was foreign to Josies's taste but she choked it down because she was hungry from working a ten-hour day. The job at the factory was boring and her hands were getting raw from holding parts under the running oil as a drill punched a hole in each part as it passed by. She couldn't help but wonder what the part was used for in the scheme of things. It didn't look like part of a bomb or plane that would contribute to the war effort.

Tonight some of the girls in her section had asked her to go with them to the Pub in town where it was rumored soldiers from a nearby army base went to dance and have a few beers. Men were scarce these days and it sure would be fun to dance again!

Josie saw him the minute she entered the bar. He was sitting quietly while those around him were gesturing, telling jokes and hoisting their glasses. His uniform was definitely not army, but it looked immaculate, the creases pressed to perfection. Most of the guys had their caps pushed back on their heads but he had removed his and it lay on the table beside him, the Marine emblem glowing. He was tapping his feet in rhythm with the music and his short brown hair that had been slicked down was trying to curl. He looked up and his eyes met hers and she felt her cheeks grow warm. His eyes were mesmerizing, hazel with specks of copper that seemed to dance as he smiled at her. His chin had a deep cleft and a dimple hovered in the corner of his cheek. Josie looked away. What must he think of her staring like that? He was getting up, coming toward her and she glanced around to see where the other girls had gone. They were sitting down at a table with a group of soldiers and suddenly he was standing in front of her.

"Hi, they just happen to be playing my favorite song. Would you care to dance?"

"I – uh- I ...my friends are sitting, I mean I haven't even sat down yet." Josie knew she must sound flustered.

"That's all right. It's casual here. I'll take you to the table after we dance, ok?"

He took her lightly in his arms and she felt as though she was floating across the dance floor. *Stardust* it was one of her favorites too and then the music stopped and they stood facing each other. "I'm Dominic Romano but my friends call me Nick"

"Same here I'm Josie, I mean Josephine, but no one calls me that except my father and my mother when she's mad at me" Her laugh was bubbly.

"I'm really glad to meet you." Nick turned and went back to his table.

Josie sat down amid her friends whistling and raised eyebrows.

"You're a fast worker." Sally was a petite girl with long dark hair. "He's pretty cute and a Marine too."

Josie felt a blush creeping across her face. "I don't know what came over me."

Sally laughed, "Hey, I was just teasing. We're all buddies here."

The following Saturday night both Nick and Josie appeared at the Pub with their friends. Nick watched Josie from a distance. Her honey colored hair just barely touched her shoulders and bounced when she laughed or turned her head. She wore a dress of midnight blue and her slim heeled pumps made her legs look long and incredibly gorgeous. Nick could hardly wait until it seemed appropriate to ask her to dance. James watched him warily. "It's that same girl. She must come here a lot."

"Probably no more than we do." Nick didn't like the implication that Josie was a regular. "I'm going over and ask her to dance."

Josie rose to meet him as he approached the table as though she'd been waiting. He took her in his arms and it was as though they had known one another forever. Their bodies melded in a perfect fit and she matched his intricate steps in a way no other girl had ever done. When the band played *In the Mood* they swung into it laughing and matching step for step until the crowd began to back away and watch. Nick swung her over his head and under his legs and the crowd clapped and cheered. When the music ended they were both flushed and breathless.

"Let's get some fresh air." Nick said and taking her by the hand led her out into the night. Stars peppered the sky and a slim crescent moon rocked gently or was that just because her head was spinning. There was a chill in the air and Nick removed his coat and wrapped it around her shoulders. He pulled her close and kissed her upturned lips. When they pulled a part it was as though the world had disappeared and they were the only people left on the planet.

"I should go back inside." Josie's voice was a mere whisper.

Nick nodded and hand in hand they went inside to join their friends.

As the days went by Nick and Josie saw each other whenever possible. Nick worked diligently learning everything possible about communication in the United States Marine Corp but since it was more a school than general duty he was able to get away most evenings for a few hours and had Sunday off.

Josie too worked long hours but was willing to spend her free time with Nick. They went to the movies, the museums and the park and had found an adorable little Italian restaurant on a side street in Little Italy where for the first time since being away from home, Nick tasted the fragrant tasty dishes of his heritage. The bread was thick and crusty and reminded him of his mother's loaves as she removed them from the oven. Josie had never eaten ethnic food except that of her landlady and she savored the wonderful tastes and smells Nick introduced.

The owner whose name was Angelo was a short rotund Italian with thick black hair sprinkled with silver and a mustache more silver than black. His accent was thick and his laugh hearty and the war seemed far away until his jukebox played the records of Kate Smith singing *God Bless America* or a sad English voice singing *The White Cliffs of Dover.* Many evenings Nick and Josie sat long after dinner sipping the deep garnet wine and dreading the time they had to part. Josie never invited Nick to Mrs. Goldman's for fear that she would gossip to Mrs. Fryman who in turn would tell her mother that she had a boyfriend and spoil the perfect love they shared.

Winter came to Michigan as it always did with a snow storm that dropped twelve inches of snow that swirled in the wind and piled drifts like castles that reached for the sky. Nick and Josie decided to find a place they could be alone that would be warm and cozy so they could talk and read and maybe even fix a simple meal. Angelo had the perfect place. A room above the restaurant that he had fixed up for a man who worked for him but had long since departed was still presentable and with a little cleaning would be a nice little get away. To Nick he said, "You be good and honorable to the young lady, yes?" He wiggled his finger.

"Of course, Angelo. You know we just want to be alone sometimes."

Angelo shook his head. He was a romantic himself and nobody's fool but they were nice kids and old enough to know what they were doing.

Josie was thrilled with their little hideaway. It had a small bed, an old overstuffed chair, a small table and a hot plate with a shelf above it that held a few dishes some spices and a coffeepot.

"We'll push the bed against the wall and make it into a day bed." Josie's voice was as enthusiastic as though she was furnishing a mansion. She put her arms around Nick's waist and looked up at him. "Our own little place so we can actually be alone with no one to see us or hear us."

Nick laughed. "You make it sound very mysterious."

The next day Josie went to Woolworth's and bought some bright colored pillows and a piece of oilcloth for the table printed with fruit of yellow, orange and green. She bought coffee and tea and biscuits and Angelo gave her an old phonograph and a few records.

Josie loved the little apartment even though the bathroom was downstairs and she had to wash in the tiny sink. Angelo had given it to them for a very small monthly fee and even that cut into her finances. She wished she could leave Mrs. Goldman's and tried to reason that she was earning her own money and should be able to live where she pleased, especially now that she was eighteen, but she knew that her mother would be very upset.

It was a Saturday afternoon and the snow was once more covering the city with white flakes that promised to stay for a while. The temperature had fallen to the lowest of the season, traffic was snarled and many businesses were closing early. Nick and Josie were warm and snug in their little hide-away while the odor of spices drifted up from the restaurant below. Nick sniffed the air. "I almost feel like I'm coming into Mama's kitchen."

"You miss your mother don't you?" Josie's voice had a touch of envy.

"Sure, don't you?"

"Not really. She's hardly ever home and we're not that close."

Nick ran his finger down Josie's cheek and kissed the tip of her nose. "That's strange, you're being alone and all."

Josie shrugged, "Yeah, well for some reason she seems to think I'm like my father or something. I've never really understood her."

Nick pulled her close to him. "How could anyone not love someone as sweet and cuddly as you?"

Josie snuggled closer. "Are you teasing me?"

"No." Nick lifted her chin and found her mouth. His tongue opened it tenderly and probed inside. He felt her nipples harden and opened her blouse. He circled her breast with his finger and she moaned softly. He dropped his head and suckled gently, she caught her breath and her fingers grasped his hair. As he moved downward she writhed beneath him and they came together in an ecstasy that neither had ever experienced. They lay still in one another's arms and their eyes met in love and wonderment. Tears of joy lay thick on her lashes and Nick could taste the saltiness as he kissed them away. They were both visibly shaken and Nick was the first to recover. He brought a warm cloth and sponged her gently while her eyes adored him.

"God, I'm starving. Let's go downstairs and have some dinner." Nick pulled Josie to her feet.

Angelo had a table ready for them. "You're just in time, my little ones. I'm going to close early before I get snowed in. There'll be very little business tonight with the warnings on the radio."

"Warnings?" Nick looked surprised. "Is the snow that bad?"

"Look outside my friend. You are lucky you can stay in. They are warning anyone not to be out unless necessary. These late winter storms can be the worst. I'm closing as soon as we can get cleaned up. I want my people to get home as well as myself. Yes, you are lucky." Angelo winked at them.

Later Nick and Josie would both remember that night as the one that changed their lives forever.

The gossip Josie had feared Mrs. Goldman would spread became reality when Mrs. Fryman told her mother that she knew for certain that Josie was spending most of her nights away. Josie wrote to her mother that she was moving into an apartment with her girlfriend and that it would be much cheaper than what she had to pay Mrs. Goldman.

Nick's school was close to being finished and he would be shipped to another location. They spent as much time as possible together and Josie felt that at last she knew true love. Like many other women she felt that she could not bear to let him go but by now they all knew that war was a time of sacrifice and she would be no different than all the other wives and girlfriends that she knew.

On the last weekend before Nick's class ended they invited James and Sally to their place for dinner. Nick arrived early with the excuse that he would help with the dinner. Angelo had given them a card table and folding chairs.

"Why can't we just eat at the restaurant?" Josie seemed puzzled and no wonder. It was very hard trying to surprise her as Nick and Angelo were finding out.

"I want Sally and James to see the place and help us celebrate."

"Celebrate what? Your leaving is hardly cause for celebration for me."

Nick took Josie by the hand and led her to the daybed. He knelt before her. "Josie I love you more than I could ever have imagined love could be and I know it's probably selfish to ask you at this time but will you wait for me and marry me when I return?"

Josie looked down at this handsome man that she so adored and her heart felt as though it would burst. Her eyes filled with tears and she held out her hand to accept the ring he took from his pocket.

"I will wait for you as long as it takes and love you forever." She slid to the floor beside him and they held each other tightly. Just then there was a knock and Sally and James came in. James looked at the couple on the floor in each other's arms. "I see we're just in time to celebrate!"

"You knew?" Josie smiled and stood up and kissed them both.

Just then Angelo came in carrying food enough for the proverbial army, two of his waiters in tow. There was turkey with all the trimmings and pasta and sauce and salad and last of all a cake decorated with roses of palest pink.

"Happy Engagement!" he said kissing Josie as he set the cake on the table already laden with food. He shook hands with Nick and slapped him on the back. "You got a prize fella, take care and come back safe."

Lieutenant Briggs called a special session of his class. As they waited for him to enter there was speculation among the men about where they were going. Some of them were itching to get into action while others had learned to like the academic atmosphere of school. They stood at attention as he entered the room.

"At ease." The Lieutenant's voice was crisp. "I want to congratulate all of you on a job well done. The Marines need communication experts and I am proud to say that you have exceeded my expectations. Today I am handing out certificates for the completion of the course. A copy will also be put in your file. Some day this may come in handy in civilian life." The Lieutenant's eyes surveyed his crew. "You will also be receiving a copy of your orders and a stripe that denotes you are now Private First Class."

Dominic swallowed the lump in his throat. Three months ago Michigan had been a foreign place to him and now he was leaving the girl he loved and had asked to be his wife. A nagging doubt formed in his mind and he wondered if it had all been too fast and if it was fair to a lonely girl like Josie to tie her down to someone who she might not see again for years. Tonight he would give her a chance to back out.

Lieutenant Briggs was still talking and Dominic heard his name. "Dominic Romano made a perfect score on his final test and will receive a pin denoting excellent skill in radio communications. Now if you will stand I will present your certificates." The men stood as one and as they were presented their certificates they saluted. When Nick's turn came he felt a surge of excitement. "Well done, private first class."

"Thank you sir," Nick responded as he saluted his officer.

"One last thing" the Lieutenant was smiling now. Your departure time is 0600 Monday morning. You have a forty-eight hour pass before you board. Don't get into trouble or miss the train. Dismissed!"

The men began milling about talking about their assignments and deciding what to do with their last few hours. "Private Romano."

The Lieutenant motioned for Nick in a casual personal way. "Could I see you in my office?"

Nick went at once and as they entered the Lieutenant seemed a different person. He tossed his cap on the desk and leaned back in his chair. "Sit down, Nick." He waved toward the other chair. "You've really done great in this field and I wanted to explain a little about your assignment."

"Camp Elliot?"

"Yes, you will be working with men who are pro's in cryptography who are now working on a new code based on the Navajo Indian language."

"Whew, that sounds pretty complicated."

"It is, but will fit perfectly with your radio skills. You will be working with the Navajo's too. I think you're really going to like it."

"It sure wasn't what I expected."

The Lieutenant stood up and shook his hand. "Good luck soldier. I'm really proud of the work you did. I was hoping I'd get someone like you in my class."

"Thank you, sir."

"I know it's none of my business, but it's come to my attention that you've become engaged, true?"

"Yes sir."

"You know, soldier, it probably seems pretty important right now but let me warn you that you've only been here a few months and you're going to be gone a long time, probably on a dangerous mission. You can't always be positive about things like that so fast so be careful, all right?"

"Yes sir."

The Lieutenant came around the desk and put his hand on Nick's shoulder. "I hope I run into you again sometime. Take care."

Nick saluted and turned on his heel the Lieutenant's words weighing on his mind.

Josie's emotions were a mixed bag. On one hand she was happy they had Nick's last two days together, but she also knew that when he left, she might not see him until the war ended. She wondered if she should tell him she was late with her period. Maybe they could get married tomorrow and she would be his legal wife. But what if instead he was angry and felt trapped and she lost him forever. She remembered him saying that he must always use a condom because the Corp didn't want a lot of little souvenir's running around. Why was it they hadn't used a condom? Josie remembered the night it must have happened. The night of the snowstorm and their passion had overtaken them and now they must face the consequences. That still did not solve her dilemma. Josie realized that it might spoil their last time together. It seemed she had been playing house for some time now. Pretending in her mind they were married. She had fixed up the apartment so cozy and broken her tie with Mrs.Goldman in spite of her mother's objection. Nick would be here any minute and Josie wanted only his love. The love she craved from her mother was nothing compared to the love she shared with Nick.

The door burst open, "Hey, I've got great news!" Nick threw his cap on the daybed and grabbed Josie around the waist. "I'm headed for San Diego and more school and I have my first stripe and a pin for top student."

"Oh Nick, I'm so proud of you." Josie took the plastic bag containing the stripes and went to find her needle and thread to sew one on his uniform. "Off with your shirt soldier and I'll make it official."

Nick sat in his undershirt watching Josie whose head was bent over his shirt. Her hair fell forward nearly covering her face. She was a wonderful girl. He wished the Lieutenant could meet her and he would know this was not some fly-by-night affair but the real thing.

"So what do you want to do for two whole days?" Nick's voice was filled with excitement and his hazel eyes with golden flecks seemed to dance.

"I'm late." Josie looked up and straight into Nick's eyes.

At first Nick looked blank and then it dawned on him what she meant.

"You can't be. I used protection."

"Maybe one time we slipped up."

"Oh my God," Nick put his head between his hands. "It can't be. It's not the right time." When he looked up the dancing flecks in his eyes were gone and they were cold.

"It's not the end of the world, Nick. I'll stay here and have the baby and wait for you."

"Are you crazy? How long do you think you can work? You'll need money." Nick's voice was as cold as his eyes. "You know I have a commitment to my mother and she gets my allotment."

Josie's eyes filled with tears. She had never heard that tone in Nick's voice and it frightened her. "I'm sorry I mentioned it. Just forget I said anything and I'll take care of it myself."

"Maybe it's just a false alarm, a mistake. You had that cold and they say sometimes that effects your cycle."

"Sure, that must be it." Josie was not one for sarcasm but it seemed warranted now. "Let's go get something to eat." She tossed his shirt to him with the black stripe neatly sewn.

The subject was closed or so it seemed. Nick and Josie met the gang at the Pub and the celebration went on until after midnight.

As they fell into bed in the early morning hour Nick kissed Josie lightly and turned his face to the wall. Josie forced back the tears that prickled behind her eyes. The small bed felt cramped. Usually they slept wrapped in each other's arms but tonight was different and she hoped not an omen of things to come.

The next morning Nick seemed like his old self and as they sipped their coffee, he announced that he was going to Mass at the big Cathedral in town. He usually went to the chapel on the base so it would be a treat.

"How about my going with you?"

"You wouldn't mind?"

"Just because I'm a Methodist doesn't mean I can't visit another church."

Nick and Josie walked out into the spring sunshine. The leaves and buds were poking out their tiny heads to receive the warm sun and birds twittered like little old ladies at sewing circle.

"I can't believe it's been a year since I graduated."

"Yeah, it's been two years for me." Nick smiled at her. "We're getting old."

The deep tones of the Cathedral bell tolled and Nick took Josie's hand and sprinted up the steps.

Josie had only been in a Catholic Church once in her life when she went to a Christmas program with a friend and she gasped as she saw the splendor of the Cathedral. Sun was filtering through the tall stain glass windows sending rainbows across the heads of the kneeling congregation. The altar of marble and gold looked miles away and was banked with flowers. As they slid into the nearest pew Nick fell on his knees, made the sign of the cross and closed his eyes in prayer. Josie was uncertain what to do but just then a bell rang and everyone rose to a great shuffling of feet. Two priests in beautiful flowing vestments trimmed in gold were preceded by two altar boys in white cassocks carrying a huge crucifix. Two more carried a large gold bible. The music that resounded from the organ stopped and all was still as the priest began to speak. After a confusing series of ups and downs, more music, a homily and more prayers nearly the whole congregation filed up the aisle to receive communion from the priests. Nick came back and knelt again in deep prayer and then at last it was over and the crowd surged to the doors. It had taken exactly one hour. The priest was standing outside and shook Nick's hand. " We're all very proud of you son. May God be with you."

"I'm starving!" Nick sounded happy, "how did you like my church?

"It's very ornate." Josie was careful not to sound critical. "I'm starved too. Let's go to the Country Kitchen and eat on the patio."

The waitress didn't look too pleased to bring their food to the patio. It was still a bit chilly for outdoor serving but since there was no one else there it was very private. When they finished breakfast and were sipping a second cup of coffee Nick leaned forward.

"Josie, I love you and want to marry you but there is no way we could do it before I leave so I want you to know that if by a remote chance you are pregnant, however you handle it, is all right with me. If it proves true, I'll help all I can financially and as soon as I'm out of the service we'll get married."

Nick had it all figured out. Josie heard the finality in his voice and wondered if God had a hand in this with all the praying he had done. She knew it was no use to argue, so she said nothing.

The silence hung like a curtain between them. Nick took her hand across the table. "I'll write every minute I get a chance and you do the same and we'll stay close, I promise."

Josie nodded her head, choking back the tears that burned her eyes.

"Well, so that's that. Let's go to a movie." It occurred to Josie that they would not have to talk and if she cried he would think it was from the movie so they spent some of their last hours in a darkened theater.

The time had come to say good-bye. Nick had finally made soft gentle love to Josie just before dawn, their passion subdued in the wake of her news and his leaving.

They stood on the sidewalk in front of the restaurant. A spring rain began to fall as the sun tried vainly to break through, turning the leaves iridescent and dripping off the brim of Nick's hat. He hugged Josie hard as she clung to him briefly then ran up the stairs.

"I love you. I'll write!" She did not turn around and Nick slung his duffel bag over his shoulder and hurried to board the train for California.

Chapter VII
Summer 1944

Nick sat on the edge of his bed writing his weekly letter to his mother and now a second one to Josie. The one to his mother was easy. He described how beautiful California looked as they came to camp through the city of San Diego. Flowers seemed to be everywhere even on the freeways, their bright blooms flowed between the lanes of traffic and in the open back of the truck the odor of flowers overtook the smell of carbonmonoxide emitting from the congestion of cars. Palm trees waved in front of white stucco buildings whose red tile roofs rose to meet them. How different they were from the houses in the coalmining town where Nick grew up. They took on the dingy gray of the coalmines that spewed their thick black smoke over everything. He closed his letter by saying that he was still in school with no orders to be shipped into action. His mother would be relieved to hear it and he could see her tucking the letter in her pocket to read over and over.

The letter to Josie was difficult to write as she had not yet informed him if she was indeed pregnant and all he could do was assure her of his love and his return to her after the war was over. He knew this was probably not enough and felt helpless. Finally he put the letter aside and went into the compound.

James and several others sat playing cards on an overturned barrel. James motioned for Nick to join them. Nick shook his head and wandered over to the young Navajo who was in the cryptography class. "Hi, mind if I join you?"

The Navajo smiled faintly, "Glad to have you. My buddy is writing to his wife and they", he nodded at the card players, "don't seem to think I'd know how to play."

"Do you?"

The Navajo laughed, "No, but it would have been good to be asked."

"I'm sorry but I'm not sure I know your name. I'm Nick Romano."

"Paul Begay" the Navajo stuck out his hand.

"That doesn't sound like an Indian name."

"That's the name on my Marine Corp application, but we have other names we go by on the reservation."

"So you'll be one of the code-talkers?"

"Yes, I'm looking forward to getting into action."

The two men enjoyed their talk and as the sun began to set, Paul walked to the far corner of the compound. His Navajo friend met him and they began a silent ritual to their Gods. Nick joined James and the others for chow, the letter to Josie forgotten.

Monday morning the Colonel appeared in front of the class. As one they stood at attention.

"At ease, men" the Colonels voice was crisp. "You will be pulling out of here at 0600 tomorrow morning." Many of the men had been waiting for this and were elated that at last they would see action. The Colonel continued, "There is one more stop before you hit the beaches. You are going to a camp in Hawaii where you will be assigned to the ship that will take you to a specific conflict." The Colonel consulted a paper in his hand.

"Privates First Class Romano and Conelly I will see you in my office." Nick and James exchanged glances. "Dismissed."

Nick and James sat in the Colonel's outer office. James wiggled restlessly. "What do ya spose we did?"

Nick grinned, "It doesn't mean we did anything wrong." James rolled his eyes.

"Romano," the secretary called, "you're up."

Nick knocked.

"Come in."

The Colonel motioned Nick to a chair dismissing his salute. "You know about the Navajo and the codes you've been working on but now I have another part of the duty that is to be top-secret. In your battalion there will be assigned only two Navajo. They must be protected at all costs. The Japanese have not been able to break this code by any means. Their only hope is to capture one of the men and torture him until he talks. The Navajo are tough and I know they would not break easily but you have no conception of their means of torture. We have decided to assign you to one of the men, namely Paul Begay and you are to protect him to the point of shooting him yourself if he falls into enemy hands."

Nick gulped and let what the Colonel said sink in. "That sounds like babysitting, sir."

The Colonel shot him a look that would shrivel any man. "Not on your life soldier. You'll be in as much danger as he will but it will be your responsibility that the code does not fall into enemy hands. Understood?"

"Yes sir."

"No one and I do mean NO one is to know that you are acting in that capacity. This is top secret all the way."

"Very good sir." Nick stood and saluted.

As he passed James on the way out Nick gave him a slight shrug. He heard the secretary call his name.

That evening Nick watched Paul and the other Navajo whose name was Sam Hawthorn as they went through their ritual to prepare for the next day's journey. He wondered how this young strong lean Indian with the dark eyes and stoic face would feel if he knew that he was being protected by a Dago from Colorado.

Chapter VIII
The Navajo

The old pick-up bounced along the road leading into the reservation and pulled up at the General Store. Paul Begay jumped out and opened the door. The old man behind the counter peered over his glasses, "Paul, good to see ya'. How's school in the big city?"

"Okay, I guess." Paul shrugged. He didn't think old man Smith really wanted to hear how it felt to be an Indian in a mostly white college. "I heard the Government sent a guy here to recruit some Indians for the Marines."

"Yeah, he's set up over at the office. Don't think he's had many takers though."

"I think I'll go talk to him. See what he's got to say." Paul waved and headed for the office.

The Marine was sitting behind a desk in full uniform and stood up when Paul entered. When he had first arrived the Navajo would have nothing to do with the mysterious recruiting team but the council chairman, Chee Dodge sent out a call for recruits over the short-wave radio. The next morning recruiters were greeted by a long line of applicants.

Most of the applicants knew nothing about the code-talking program but were told they would be trained as "specialists". Some even confused the word Marine with sub-marine and thought they would be trained for underwater duty.

Paul heard about the program when he saw a notice on the bulletin board at school and was intrigued but he was also cautious. The tales told to him by the elders were forever part of his thinking. No matter that the priest at the mission school had tried to expunge those thoughts and deeds from his very soul. He knew how his ancestor's had suffered but he also knew that if this country known as the United Stated were to fall into enemy hands, especially those with yellow skin and slanted eyes, it could be a fate far worse than any that had gone before. Paul's education had brought with it a greater understanding of the world. Paul approached the Sergeant and shook his hand.

"What exactly will this program entail?" The Sergeant looked up quickly at the young Navajo who stood tall and lean before him. His black hair was pulled back in a thick braid but he wore blue jeans and a neat white shirt. He was just what the program needed.

"The U.S. needs more than anything an unbreakable code. The Japs seem to know our every move and they are running the show. We've got to find a way to communicate with our men in the field or we're sunk".

"You're going to use our language as a code?"

"Right. We have a white man who speaks your language and he'll work it out with you."

"It's not a written language."

"Understood, but this will all be done by radio."

"They will teach us how to do this?"

"You betcha', so will you sign up?"

"Yes and perhaps my friend will sign too. I will tell him of it."

"Good." The Sergeant pushed the paper toward him. Paul read it in its entirety, then stood up and extended his hand.

"We'll be in touch." The Sergeant nodded and Paul walked away.

That evening the sun turned a brilliant orange as it slipped from sight behind the sculptured rock that loomed above the reservation. Paul sat quietly until the stars filled the sky and a sliver of moon appeared to join the nightly playground. His thoughts had been deep and as in the old ways he had asked the spirits for guidance. He rose slowly and began to pick his way through the tumbled cactus, still thinking of his conversation with the sergeant. As he entered the hogan his mother Singing Bird looked up from her beading.

"Are you hungry my son?" She did not seem surprised to see him and he wondered if the chain of gossip that flitted like a bee from flower to flower had already informed her of his coming. If so, she probably also knew why he had come and where he had stopped.

"No, I spoke to the recruiter who has come to the reservation." His mother's fingers stopped moving and a shadow of fear flickered across her smooth face.

"You forget what they did to your father?" Her voice filled with the sadness of many moons.

"It is a new generation, a new war against one that attacked us and killed thousands and will not stop until our country can find a new way to stop them. We Navajo may be that way."

"Humph." The guttural sound came from deep within. "They do not keep their word." Paul touched her shoulder lightly.

"Hopefully it will be different this time."

His mother went back to her work with a slight shake of her head.

Paul left the hogan and whistled for his friend Sam Running Horse. He emerged silently out of the darkness. Together they walked to the edge of the canyon and sat cross-legged on the barren ground.

"I signed up today," Paul said softly. "They say we will be specialists."

Running Horse nodded, "It is our duty."

He was short of stature but strong and muscular. He was dressed in the soft skins of his ancestors and had been like a big brother to Paul all their lives. "I will leave my squaw and sons in the good hands of her father."

Running Horse had many thousands of sheep and his father-in-law and sons would care for them until he returned. The two stood as brothers, their hands on one another's shoulder, and the pact was made. They would go together.

The following day Paul went to the hogan to call on Morning Star. They had been playmates as children and their friendship had ripened into love as they matured. She sat outside, her hands busily forming a clay pot. Her fingers seemed to move in a rhythm all their own as the design took form. Her pots were in great demand and once he had asked her how she decided on a pattern and she had answered. "I don't know until my heart tells my fingers what to do."

Her long black hair fell across her shoulders and partially hid her face. Paul spoke quietly so as not to startle her. "I have come to say good-bye."

Morning Star rose gracefully and wiped her hands. Her dark eyes and the smooth planes of her face and high cheekbones gave no hint of surprise. She motioned Paul inside. There on a soft woolen blanket she pulled him to her and began to undress him. Slowly she unbuttoned his shirt and slid it off his shoulders, then undid his jeans and let them slide to the floor. When he was naked she removed her own woven cotton gown with its colorful beading and looked deeply into his eyes. Paul's heart was thumping as she ran her slim fingers over his body and enfolded him to her breast. Paul's body seemed to float away and he tasted her lips and nibbled her ear and let his tongue run over the smooth skin to the small hollow of her throat. Their bodies seemed weightless and fragile with no beginning and no end. When at last they lay still, bathed in the sweat of their passion, she said in a tremulous whisper, "I will wait for you, my love."

"I will return." Paul's voice was hushed.

She pressed into his hand a soft buckskin pouch containing herbs to ward off the evil spirits and white corn to keep him safe. She whispered a blessing in his ear as soft and gentle as the wind and with that she led him outside, turned and disappeared.

The tales of horror in boot camps were not exaggerated and young Navajo boys who were used to running free were suddenly under the command of hard-nosed screaming *beleganna* sergeants who ordered them about at will. For the most part the Navajo took the officers abuse in stride. In fact the impossibility of riling up the Navajos drove the drill instructors to despair. Long marches meant nothing to the Navajo who had lived under harsh conditions for years. They were used to going without food, sleeping on the ground and even obtaining water from the desert plants when the canteens became empty. They became known as super human creatures.

Paul and Sam were amused at the sergeants who tried to be so tough and when they were alone they talked of many things. Paul had missed their talks when he went away to school but Sam understood that Paul was different and would never be happy just raising sheep. He wanted to be a teacher and show the young people that there were other worlds, other opportunities that they could pursue. As for Sam, he was content to live by the old ways. The days went by quickly and then boot camp was over and it was time to go to another place to learn their craft.

The Navajo were sent to Camp Pendelton to learn the techniques of communicating messages. They studied Morse code, semaphore signals, military message writing, wire laying, pole climbing and were trained in the operation of radios that would be used in combat zones. Even though the Navajo had no experience in electronics they had to learn how to take apart and put together the bulky field radios and to care for them so they would not break or malfunction.

The most important task was to develop the code. They had to learn page after page of military terminology from all branches. Their mission was to create a Navajo equivalent for each word. In order to maintain secrecy nothing could be written down and everything would be committed to memory. It took weeks of grueling work. Sam Running Horse who had little formal schooling did extremely well in all aspects and it made Paul very proud of his friend.

The American Marines arrived in camp to work with the Navajo on the last stage of planning. They were already adept at communication, laying wire, repairing broken parts and generally keeping the gear in shape but they were not to be given the actual code. Only the Navajo were to have that secret knowledge.

Paul and Sam were not comfortable with the Marines who called them *Chief* and treated them like second class citizens. This was *their* mission and the American hotshots didn't even realize that it was the Navajo who were the really important ones. The Navajo had been told that as soon as the mission was completed, they would receive a promotion in rank. Unfortunately once again the U.S. government broke their promise and refused to confer the rank of first class on the Navajo. Even those men who were retained as instructors for the next batch of recruits were denied a promotion.

The Colonel handed out the orders that would take the new platoon to Hawaii for the last two weeks of simulated battle conditions before sending them into combat and the real war.

The Colonel could only hope that the Navajo and the white soldiers would work together in this important assignment and make it a truly American team.

Chapter IX
Michigan

Josie woke stiff and groggy at the sound of the alarm. She pulled herself up from the daybed still dressed in the same clothes she had worn the day before. She felt empty, not hungry but completely empty as though her insides had been hollowed out. Her brain too seemed frozen, unable to concentrate. Josie made herself go down the narrow wooden steps to the bathroom. She washed her face and armpits in the cold water and brushed her teeth. She picked up the comb from the edge of the sink, inhaled the odor of Nick's hair, the way it smelled when he buried his head in her neck.

Josie entered the factory's main room acknowledging the greetings with a wave of her hand. She sat down at her machine and turned it on. The pungent smell of oil sliding down the trough to lubricate the drill entered her nostrils and sent waves of nausea to her empty stomach. She took a small circle of steel from the pile next to the drill and centered it perfectly as the drill punched a hole. It was a mindless job and Josie hated it but for once she was glad not to have to think. Suddenly she felt a wave of nausea so intense it brought bitter bile to the back of her throat. Quickly she shut off the machine and raced to the lavatory. She barely made it to the porcelain bowl before the watery vomit gushed from her throat. Josie had not eaten the night before but the spasms continued. She was on her knees and leaned her cheek against the cold porcelain.

"Are you all right in there?"

Turning her head Josie saw the black pumps with silver buckles and grey stockings of her supervisor beneath the door.

"Uh, huh." Josie's voice was hoarse.

"I've made out a pass for you to see the nurse. You look ill and your work is slipping."

Josie slid back the lock and stood facing Mrs. Beasley. She was aware of how she must look in her rumpled clothes and a piece of toilet tissue clutched in her hand.

"Be sure the nurse fills in the time. If she thinks you should go home, feel free to do so. You'll be docked of course. Mrs. Beasley turned, her heels clicking on the tile floor.

The door opened and Sally peeked in, "Are you ok?"

"I guess so. Maybe I have the flu."

"You should go home and get some rest."

"I have to see the nurse first, then I'll go home."

"Good."

Josie covered her face with her hands. "Oh Sally, I think I'm pregnant!"

Sally put her arm around her friend. "Oh no! Does Nick know?"

Josie shook her head. "I tried to tell him before he left but he said he always used protection."

"Oh sure, it's never their fault. Go on to the nurse and I'll come over tonight and we'll talk, ok?"

Josie choked back a sob and nodded. Sally gave her a hug and they walked out together.

The nurse was cool and professional as she handed Josie the results of the pregnancy test.

"You were right, you are pregnant. Is it a soldier?"

Josie felt a flush spreading across her face. "Yes, but don't think it was just a one night stand."

The nurse permitted a faint smile to flicker across her lips. Josie continued. "We love each other. We're going to be married. He gave me this." She extended her finger with the small diamond that sparkled under the fluorescent light.

"So did he leave then?"

"Yes, he's in California. He's in communications and his work is very secret."

The nurse nodded not unkindly. "It may be a long time before you see him again. Here is the address of a home for unwed mothers run by the Sisters of Charity. They will take care of you for what ever you're able to do and when the baby arrives, they'll place it with a loving family."

Josie stuffed the piece of paper in her pocket and with her lips tightly closed in a straight line, she turned toward the door.

"You can continue to work here until you begin to show," the nurse called to her receding back. "I'll send the report to Mrs. Beasley." The door slammed shut.

Josie and Sally had eaten dinner at Angelo's and now sat side by side on the daybed where Josie and Nick had talked and made love so many times.

"You need to get out of this place," Sally observed, "it's too full of memories."

"Yeah, but they're mostly good. I'll be ok."

"I brought an address for you. One of the girls in our rooming house had an abortion one Friday and was back to work on Monday."

"An abortion?" Josies's blue eyes widened. "Isn't that against the law?"

Sally sighed. "Don't be naïve. It's done all the time, especially since the war."

"I-uh really want to wait 'til I hear from Nick."

"That's just it, you can't wait too long."

Josie jumped up. "Let's go to a movie!" She put the two pieces of paper on the table anchored by a vase.

Sally shrugged. "Ok, but if you need me you know where I am."

The girls linked arms and went out into the darkness.

Josie continued to work, controlling her nausea with crackers and 7-up. She didn't dare get fired until she made some decisions. She checked the mail expectantly for some word from Nick. Finally it came. She tore open the envelope as she took the stairs two at a time and sat down to read.

My dearest Josie,

Life here is very busy. If communication school seemed hard, all this about code is even harder. I can't explain much as it is very secretive.

How I wish I could show you California. It is so warm and the ocean is as blue as your eyes. There are flowers everywhere [except on the base] and palm trees are the strangest sort of tree I've ever seen. When we get married I want to bring you here for our honeymoon. Wouldn't that be great?

I love you so much and miss our little apartment and snuggling with you. Please pray for me that I will get through this so we can be together forever. We are leaving for Hawaii and then combat. They might censor this but just know I love you and carry your picture close to my heart. With all my love, Nick

Josie stared at the paper as tears streamed from her eyes. She wadded the letter into a ball and threw it across the room. All that sweet talk and not one word about the baby! Obviously it meant nothing to him, yet it consumed her whole life.

Finally when her tears dried and darkness pushed its way into every corner, she turned on the lamp and saw the two pieces of paper lying on the table. So that's the way it's going to be. With a deep sigh she put them in her purse.

Josie had never felt really loved or at least since she was old enough to give it much thought. She tried to remember how it had been when she was small and her father had lived with them. She had never once seen her mother and father acting affectionate with one another but surely they must have loved her when she was a baby. She tried to recall the feel of her mother's lap or the sound of her voice. She did recall later when she was old enough to run and Daddy had chased her across the damp grass, in and out of the bushes, heavy with clusters of fragrant flowers, until she fell on the ground laughing. Daddy's laugh was deep and robust and he pulled up her dress and tickled her tummy and pinched her bottom until she was out of breath from giggling. She could still hear her mother's shrill voice cutting through the sunny day.

"Stop that nonsense right now and get in here."

The laughter stopped and Daddy picked her up, smoothed her dress, brushed away the blades of grass, then slung her over his shoulder and took her back to her mother.

Josie remembered her Grandma too. She had a lap as soft as a feather pillow that you could burrow in while she read you stories and sang songs. Sometimes when they visited, Daddy would sing songs of the "old sod" he called them and he and Grandma would blend their voices in "Mother McCree" while Josie clapped her hands.

One day her mother told her that Grandma had gone to heaven. She took all the songs and laughter with her. Grandpa, who had always seemed so gruff was now an old man crying into a bandana handkerchief and except for an occasional cough and sniffle the house was silent and creepy.

Not long after that Mother and Josie moved into the silent house. Mother said Grandpa needed someone to cook and take care of him. Josie did not like the house without Grandma in it and for sure didn't want to live there. Daddy didn't seem to like it either and went away to live in the city.

After what seemed like a long time things got better. Josie met new friends at school, Mother got a job and Grandpa no longer cried but the house was never the same without Grandma and Daddy's singing and laughter.

Josie felt the new life growing inside her and dreamed of bringing a baby into a world of happiness and love. Now her world was shattered. Nick, whom she loved with all her heart, wanted no part of them. Josie knew she could never bring a baby into a world without the love of both parents.

Josie stepped off the bus close to the destination on the piece of paper. Following the numbers, she came to a door with peeling paint and a rusty number. She opened the door and a bell sounded. Josie wished she had brought Sally along for moral support but she wanted to be independent and was used to being alone so she squared her shoulders and took a deep breath. Three girls sat on shabby chairs in the drab room. A blond with long stringy hair and sad gray eyes sat curled up, a plaid blanket covering her shivering body. A glass of orange juice sat on the table beside her. The other two girls talked in hushed tones, their chairs pushed close together.

Josie stood in front of the desk, piled high with papers, a typewriter and a telephone. The door behind the desk opened and a young woman, her hair frizzed in a full-blown Afro with a tight skirt and sweater and spiked heels spoke.

"You the one who called earlier?"

"Yes."

"Fill out this paper and bring it back to me."

Josie took the pen and paper and scanned the contents.

1.How many weeks since your last period?

2.Have you had any pre-natal care?

3.Married? Biological father.

4.*Next of kin.*
5.*Notify in case of emergency.*

Josie filled out the paper after hesitating over some of the answers. Her name and phone number was at the top of the paper but she left the third and fourth questions blank. She put Sally's phone number for the emergency and handed it back to the woman. A moan sounded from behind the door followed by a sharp cry. Josie felt a chill course through her body.

"There's one ahead of you." The woman nodded toward the chairs. "Here's a brochure from Planned Parenthood so's maybe you won't let this happen again. Leave the money on the desk on your way in."

"Thank you."

The brochure showed an embryo at four weeks. The caption under the next picture said a*t eight weeks the embryo becomes a fetus, fully formed with all organs in place.* Josie stared at the tiny creature curled into a ball. A lump formed in her throat and her stomach churned. She threw the brochure on the table and rushed outside. Josie hugged the lamp post as it formed a circle of light around her. She wiped away tears with her sleeve feeling a terrible revulsion to think she had almost destroyed a precious life.

The bus driver stopped and opened his door. "Ya gettin' on lady?"

Josie scrambled on the bus and slid into the nearest seat. As the distance widened she grew calmer. *There has to be a better solution.*

Saturday morning dawned bright and beautiful. Birds chirped merrily and even the dogs barked their greetings on a happy note. Josie was encouraged that she had been strong enough to make a decision on her own and was positive she could come up with a plan. She knew that to go see the Sisters at Queen of Heaven would be almost as bad as her experience at the doctors. They would want her to sign over the baby and never see it again. She had to think of a better idea than that. I'll write Mother a letter and go home until the baby's born. There's plenty of room and I've got the money I saved for the doctor. Why hadn't she thought of that before? She pulled a piece of paper from the drawer and began to write.

Dear Mother,

I have some surprising news to share with you. I am going to have a baby. The father is Nick, a soldier. He's very handsome and smart. He gave me a beautiful ring but he was shipped out before we had time to get married. I would like to come home and have my baby if it's all right. I have saved some money and will pay my own way.

Love, Josie

She ran to the corner mailbox and posted it before she changed her mind.

The factory was buzzing with the news that at last the American troops were beginning to make some headway capturing those tiny seemingly inconsequential islands on the path to Tokyo. It was reported that some new method of communication was confounding the Japanese who had previously been able to break into every message sent by the American troops.

Josie secretly knew that it was Nick and his platoon that were responsible for this remarkable feat. Oh, Nick my darling Nick if only he would write or send some sign that he knew her situation. Her anger that he had not mentioned the baby had disappeared in light of Sally's admonishment that their letters had probably crossed paths what with his moving about the war zone and mail delivery being what it was. It gave her hope that Nick would be happy about the news and anxious to end this war and come back to her.

Josie waited hopefully for word from her mother that she could move back home to await the birth of the baby. The letter arrived at last and Josie tore it open at once.

Dear Josephine,

> *I was not surprised to hear your so-called news. I was sure something like this would happen if you moved out of Mrs. Goldman's place. That was the idea of having you under motherly protection. I knew you were too young and inexperienced to be on your own. You have disappointed me for the last time. You will have to work something out as I feel it would be very inconvenient to have you here. Your grandfather is not well and I do not need any more stress. I hope it works out for you, but I'm afraid you may just have ruined any chance at the life I was hoping for you. Good Luck,*
> *Mother*

Josie stared at the letter as though she could change the terse message it contained but of course she could not. She dropped the letter and pulled a bright orange pillow into her arms and curled up in a ball, hugging it close to her heart.

Chapter X
Island Hopping

As they left Hawaii for combat there was a certain excitement aboard the ship that had never been present before. All of the men knew that at last they were going into the real thing. The ammunition would be real and there would be no second chances to get it right. All they had learned would be put to the test and the results would be life and death.

As they plowed through the waters of the Pacific, they expected to see carriers and hospital ships and hear the roar of Air Force planes, but all seemed eerily quiet and they saw only one hospital ship as they neared the tip of the island.

The Colonel called for a briefing and hundreds of green young troops outfitted for war stood at attention on the deck of the ship.

"At ease," the Colonel shouted and the men slouched, some going so far as to sit or lean against the bulkhead. We will be dropping you men here and you will make camp and get set up and at 0400 aircraft from Henderson field will cover you. Our troops have plenty of equipment set up and you'll see as soon as you land. The Island is cut in two and it's your job to squeeze the enemy from both sides into a trap. All your training will come to you once you find yourself in the situations we practiced. There will also be plenty of seasoned men to help show you the ropes. Are we ready?"

The men rose in unison, shouting and raising their guns in the air. The small amphibious boats were lined up and the men clamored aboard. They would still have to wade the last few yards but they were definitely on their way.

The men in their heavy gear jumped into the water and headed for shore. Nick saw Sam's heavy radio pack drag the water. Paul saw it too and hiked it up as Sam turned and gave him a grateful look. The water was warm and filled with debris and stunk to high heaven. As they neared the shore shots came from the east direction but were answered quickly by the Marines already dug in position.

The new men plowed on and were greeted with shouts.

"Bout time ya got here!" and " Where ya been, greenies?"

They were slapped on the back and hugged by burly men who were unwashed and unshaven but also cautioned to hunker down and be quiet until four AM when the aircraft would cover them and they went on the offensive.

Nick turned to the soldier next to him. "How do you know where the Japs are?"

"Ya don't. We know most of 'em are holed up on the East shore of the island and that's where we'll head, but they could be anywhere. They're sneaky devils and they can burrow in the ground and jump up any time."

Nick felt his heart thump and knew his palms were sweating. He looked at Paul who seemed unperturbed and wondered how he could protect him. Everything was so quiet you could not imagine how or when things would erupt. He knew they were to wait until the proper time when they would be the ones to start the action, but what if the Japs decided to start shooting first? Nick took a small sip from his canteen and found it hard to swallow.

"Jesus, this is it?" James sounded incredulous. "I thought we'd be in the thick of it."

"We will." Nick nodded at the soldier next to him. "He says they can pop up anywhere. I'm worried how we're going to keep track of our Indians."

Paul must have heard the word "Indian" and looked at Nick from across the group. A slight sardonic smile gave Nick the impression that he was more than able to take care of himself.

Darkness came swiftly in the jungle and most of the men tried to catch a few winks. There had been no prepared food and they had nibbled from their kits but no one seemed hungry. The waiting seemed interminable and Nick wondered if the Japanese were waiting too. Were they young and green or were they, as he had heard, so dedicated to their Emperor that their own life meant nothing.

In the still night filled only with occasional sounds of animals, a distant drone could be heard. Nick saw the men tense and suddenly out of the quiet came the deep voice of the Sergeant. "Charge!"

The men rose and began to creep forward and suddenly the gray dawn was filled with the sound of gunfire. Huge tanks were moving out and Japanese shouts filled the air. The planes were overhead and bombs came from everywhere. Bullets and grenades lit up the sky as the men waded through the tangled vines and brush. Nick tried to keep Paul in his sight but it was nearly impossible as Paul sashayed back and forth shooting at every mound of dirt. From these mounds came screams as Japs with guns pointed, went down backward. This seemed to keep up endlessly. Every Japanese nest that was blown up seemed to have another one right behind it. Paul was still in front of him and Nick knew that was not the way it was supposed to be. He should be the one in front. Just then a Jap jumped up in front of Paul, his tommy-gun pointed straight at him. Nick could see the Jap's face but couldn't shoot because Paul was in front of him. Nick moved slightly to the left and shot just as the Jap pulled the trigger. The bullet went wild. Blood spurted from his throat as Nick's bullet went through his body. Paul looked back at Nick and with a slight tip of his finger he shoved back his helmet and a brief smile thanked Nick. The smell of blood was everywhere and finally the shooting stopped and there seemed to be no soldiers in sight. The men cheered and the Sergeant nodded at Paul who set up his radio and sent the message that sounded like gibberish but in Navajo meant they had taken the hill.

For the time being all seemed quiet and Paul searched for Sam. He found him sitting quietly beside his radio. He too had sent a message from the other platoon. When he saw Paul his face lit up. "There is so much death, I'm glad we are both safe."

Paul nodded. "What do they do with all these bodies?"

Sam shook his head. "It is not the way of the *Dineh*."

"My *belegaana* bodyguard saved my life today." Paul's voice was low and the two Navajo clasped hands and Paul went back to his own unit.

Nick sat on the ground and thought of the face of the Jap he had killed. He looked fierce but also very young and there was a flash of fear in his eyes as he fell. Nick knew that he had killed many others with all the shooting but this had been the only one who he had been close enough to see his face. He had never killed anyone before and he felt sick. Just then Paul came up to him. "Thanks for what you did today."

Nick felt a rush of gratitude that God had given him the courage to do what had to be done, but couldn't help feeling that there should be another way.

The Island was secure and now they would go on to the next island in the chain that would lead them to Tokyo.

The next Island in the chain was Iwo Jima and it was to be an all out assault. They could use the last island captured for an air and supply base for the next attack. That was what the Marines were used for. It would also need to make use of the Navajo code-talkers as communication was a prime ingredient. The last campaign had convinced the officers in command that this new form of code was working.

The American planes and naval batteries would open the assault by pounding the island with bombs and artillery shells, then the Marines could approach from the sea in their landing craft.

Nick sat hunched on the deck as the ship plowed through the waters toward Iwo Jima. His thoughts and emotions were mixed as he tried to make sense of the war and his relationship with Josie. Mail call when they arrived on the ship was the first mail since Hawaii and Josie's letter that said she was definitely pregnant had been a blow that hit hard. He had brushed off her suspicion when she was late because he had always been so careful. Damn! He closed his eyes and could see the fighting, bodies, and blood, the smells and sounds of war. He tried to see Josie, her honey colored hair, the deep blue of her eyes and how they sparkled when she was happy and darkened when she was serious. How could he help her from here? He couldn't think about it now. She would have to handle it!

Paul slid down beside Nick. "Ready to go eat?"

"Not really, I don't feel hungry."

"It may be the last decent meal before we land and are eating K-rations again."

"Okay, you sold me."

The two men joined the others as they crowded into the mess hall.

The gray dawn was eerily quiet as the landing craft pulled up to the ship. The men had been cautioned to not speak unless absolutely necessary and to move slowly so the sound would not carry across the still water. The only sound was that of the birds chirping as they fluttered from one tree to another disturbed by an invasion of their privacy. Wave after wave of men moved toward the shore. Nick and Paul stayed close together as Paul struggled to keep his equipment out of the water and Nick held his rifle high and kept his left hand on a grenade in his pocket. The water was warm and putrid as they strode toward shore. They had been fooled before by these sneaky bastards and this time they would be prepared. As the landing craft moved out of sight and more men hit the beach there was a sudden barrage of sound. Bombs exploded against the gray sky that was already streaked with blue and gold. Screaming Japs rose from nowhere shooting assault weapons in every direction. Men fell on their bellies and began returning fire but the bombs were sending body parts flying. Nick pushed Paul to the ground covering him with his body as he threw the grenade. They lay still trying to position themselves. Suddenly their own planes were swooping down and dropping bombs on the dense jungle. Chaos was everywhere but as the bombers headed back to the carrier, the enemy gunfire was silenced as quickly as it had begun and the Japs disappeared into the jungle.

The water behind them had turned a dirty red and the men began to pull their remaining fallen companions onto the beach. The sergeant was barking orders and they headed to the prearranged campsite leaving the dead behind. After dark they would come back, remove the dog tags and bury the bodies.

Paul finished his report and came to where Nick sat cleaning his gun.

"There were only nine men killed and fifteen injured. It seemed like more than that at the time."

"That's too many. Are James and Sam okay?"

"Yeah, they're set up on the other ridge. They lost four from their group."

"This is only the beginning. I wonder how long it'll take to secure this island."

"There's a hell of a lot of Japs here. The good thing is that we're really close to Japan so the rumor is that "Fat Man" is ready and once it's dropped, it's all over!"

" You learn a lot of stuff from that radio, don't you?. Is that the rumor about the atom bomb?"

"It's more than a rumor. They've tested it in the desert. In fact the smaller one called "Little Boy" killed everything in sight for over a hundred miles."

"Shit! That beats the way we're doing it here."

"They've even picked the cities and the bomber that'll carry it, but we still have to take these islands for supplies for the carriers."

Nick shook his head, "I just hope we survive that long."

Nick and Paul hankered down in the foxhole to catch a few winks of needed rest, each with his own thoughts to keep him company.

It was early spring of 1945 and the battles continued to rage. The men were exhausted and discouraged. The Japanese seemed to have an endless supply of young men willing to die for their Emperor.

The risk was great to call the men together in one area, but the commanding General had done just that. They stood at attention sensing something of importance. The General spoke.

" This morning, April 12th, 1945 we have been informed that President Franklin Delano Roosevelt has died at his retreat in Warm Springs, Georgia. The vice president will now become our commander-in-chief. May God Bless America. Company dismissed." He saluted and strode back to headquarters.

The men were stunned and looked at one another in disbelief. Most of them had not known any other president. He represented everything about America and home. Would this change anything? Who was this vice-president? Could he lead America? Talk broke out among the soldiers but the sergeants were taking charge, sending the men back to their own units. The war would go on as usual.

Morale was low and the enemy seemed to sense it and intensified their attack. Nick and Paul were moving close to the ground and as the gunfire surrounded them they dived into a hole. A large black man startled by their arrival jumped up and fired at Paul. Nick watched in horror as his friend recoiled and fell at his feet.

Nick pointed his gun at the soldier. "Drop your weapon! Now! You stupid son-of-a-bitch!"

The black man did as he was told. His huge eyes filled with fear.

"I uh, uh I thought he was a Jap!" His voice broke as he saw the Corporal kneel over his friend.

"Paul, oh Paul." Nick tore open his shirt and saw the wound filling with blood. Paul's eyes opened "What happened?"

"Don't talk" Nick took a rag from his pack to stench the blood. Paul's eyes closed again. Nick looked up at the soldier who looked scared with tears running down his cheeks. God, he was just a kid. "Help me get him back to the medics."

They stayed low and carried Paul to the clearing. The medic met them and took charge as Nick turned to the soldier. "What in the hell were you doing?"

"My name's Washington, suh, Calvin Washington. I got lost from my unit. There was bullets flyin' everywher'. I found that hole and jumped in. I didn't know where I was. When I saw him, he looked like a Jap and I jus' fired."

"I'll report this." Nick's voice was grim. "You new here?"

"Yes suh. We jus' landed las' night."

"For your information he is a native American, you got that?"

Nick took a pad from his pocket and wrote down the soldier's name and serial number. He felt sick. His heart ached for Paul but he could understand how this could happen. Hell, it could happen to anybody. He hurried back to check on Paul and then would report this to the sergeant.

Paul lay pale and still on the narrow cot. The medic was mixing something in a small bowl.

"How is he?"

"I think he'll make it. The shot was below the heart but a fragment is lodged in the upper part of his arm. The doctor will be here tonight. He'll probably move him to the hospital ship."

"He's a radio man and we really need him."

The medic shrugged his shoulders "So? Look man, it happens."

Nick turned away. He tried to hold back the tears that stung his eyes. Paul was like a brother to him. They couldn't be separated now. Damn this war!

The next day all hell broke loose. U.S. planes dropped bombs behind enemy lines scattering the enemy in every direction. Marines on the ground took the opportunity to shoot anything that moved. Nick hated this kind of warfare. He wondered how many of their own men were caught in the fire. No wonder the sergeant had not seemed too concerned over the incident with Paul. The whole damn war was crazy. The fighting continued until at last it was quiet. Bodies were laying everywhere enemy and friends side by side. A group of Marines were raising the flag on the knoll named Mt. Sabuci. Nick watched as the soldiers exchanged the small flag for a larger one as the men cheered. It was over at last and the island belonged to the United States of America.

Nick went in search of Sam and James. He had to tell Sam that Paul was injured and he had not seen his friends in nearly two weeks. The chaplain was making the rounds comforting those who were injured and praying over the dead. Nick waited patiently until the priest rose from giving the last rights to a soldier who appeared to have both legs blown away.

"Father Joe, excuse me for bothering you but I wonder if you have seen James and the Navajo radio man, Sam?"

Father Joe looked tired as he recognized Nick. He shook his head sadly. "I'm sorry Nick, they were both killed when a bomb exploded while Sam was sending a message."

This time Nick could not control his tears and fell on his knees and sobbed. Father Joe knelt beside him. "I'm sorry, Nick. I wish there was something I could do but the only thing I know is to pray for the souls of these beautiful young men and for their families." He blessed Nick, made the sign of the cross and moved on.

Nick went back to camp. All was eerily quiet. Most of the men who had been injured were carried on gurneys to the hospital ship and another detail was burying the dead. Nick took a wrinkled pack of cigarettes from his pocket and searched for a match. Suddenly a flame flared in his face and he looked up to see the Sergeant holding a silver lighter. He dragged on the cigarette.

"Sorry about the Navajo. He's a good man and you made a great team."

"His name is Paul, Paul Begay. He's my friend, not just some Navajo Indian."

The Sergeant turned away. Nick felt the tears rising in his throat and behind his eyes. He could smell smoke and diesel fuel and rotting flesh. He dragged heavily of the stale tobacco and felt it fill his lungs and seep through his body.

Nick lay in the bunk of the ship taking the soldiers to Hawaii. After a short rest they would be reassigned. He thought about Josie and wondered if she was all right. *I'm so sorry that I couldn't take care of you.* He counted the months he had been gone and realized that if she had been pregnant when he left she would have given birth by now. He thanked God over and over for protecting him and promised that he would write to her and do anything he possibly could to help her.

When he thought of their lovemaking he felt a growing hardness between his legs. God, it had been so long since he had held her or kissed her soft lips or felt her nipples harden in his mouth. God must have saved him for her. He reached under the rough sheet and relieved himself and in the bitter ecstasy of the moment he could feel her body and smell her hair and then it was gone and he lay alone in the hard bunk.

They landed in Hawaii and as soon as he was assigned his bed and briefed by the sergeant Nick headed out to find what had happened to Paul. The General agreed to see him and he stood before him and saluted.

"At ease soldier." The General's desk was cluttered and his gray hair was mussed as though he had run his fingers through it many times. "What can I do for you?"

" I must find out what happened to my friend. He is a Navajo code-talker and I was assigned to protect him. He was shot by one of our own men and I've got to know how he is and where."

"Sit down. What is this about being shot by one of our own soldiers?"

Paul explained the situation and ended by saying "and so you see, we're like brothers and I have to find him."

The General ran his fingers through his hair and sighed deeply. "Christ, it isn't enough that we have the Japanese fanatics but now they have us so confused we're shooting our own men." He shuffled the papers on his desk. "Give me his full name and yours too and come back at 1600 and I'll have some sort of answer for you."

"Thank you sir."

Nick stood and saluted and went out under the clear Hawaii sky. He walked to the water's edge and knelt on the white sand, "God please spare my brother and care for my Josie."

He made the sign of the cross and rose from his knees and headed toward his bunk to read the mail that had been passed out when he first arrived. The Sergeant had advised him not to try and see the General but he was very thankful that he had not taken his advice. Some times you just had to go straight to the top.

Nick was surprised to find that only one of his letters was from Josie. It was dated over six months ago. Six months! God where had the time gone?

My dearest,

I don't know when you will receive this letter but I want you to know that everything worked out for me. My grandfather died and I went to his funeral and my Aunt Leah was also there. I had not told her that I was pregnant and of course she was surprised. My Grandfather had left the house to my mother and my aunt and my mother considered this rather unfair since she had taken care of him for several years. My aunt signed papers giving up all claim to the house so it is my mothers alone. I thought in view of this that my mother might let me come home and have the baby but she said for the first time she would be able to do as she pleased and I would spoil that by bringing an illegitimate baby into the house.

My aunt was so shocked at her attitude, she promptly went with me to Grand Rapids, helped me pack up my things and brought me to New York. My uncle also welcomed me with open arms and so I was saved!

Our baby boy was born on the first day of March. He has your eyes, hair and above all a tiny cleft in his chin exactly like

yours. I hope you will love him as much as I love you both.
Yours always, Josie.
   P.S. My address is enclosed. J.

Nick felt the tears that had threatened all day coursing down his cheeks. It was already July. His baby was four months old. He buried his face in the pillow. He might have to go back to duty and God only knew what might happen. The war was supposed to end. What had happened to the big bomb that Paul had told him about. Was President Truman committed to dropping it? Would it be too late for him?

Promptly at 1600 Nick appeared at the General's office. A beautiful woman in full uniform took his name and he paced back and forth until the woman nodded for him to go in. The General waved him to a chair.

"Let's dispense with formalities Corporal. You'll be happy to hear that I have your information and it is really not that bad." He sounded almost relieved as though he had dreaded the alternative. "Your friend Private Begay is in a hospital in San Diego. My secretary will give you the name and address. His condition is fair. Actually he is in good condition except for his left arm which has so far been rendered useless."

"Useless? What does that mean?"

"I'm sorry, son, I suppose the word is paralyzed. The therapists are working with him in hopes of retaining some use of it. It seems the bullet severed the nerves and no surgery was able to correct it."

"I see."

"I have some good news for you. You will be receiving a thirty-one day leave beginning as soon as you have been processed."

"Thank you sir. I really appreciate your help and will go to see my friend as soon as possible. I also have been informed I have a son born while I was on duty and hopefully with that much leave I'll be able to see him." Nick stood and saluted.

"Congratulations! It's been a pleasure meeting you son. Good luck on all counts."

For the first time in many months Nick felt relief and a measure of happiness almost too good to be true.

The hospital in San Diego was the largest one Nick had ever seen. When he finally found the right floor and area where Paul was located, he stopped at the desk to be sure. The nurse at the desk was a petty officer and very attractive.

"I'm looking for Private Paul Begay." Nick looked at the long line of beds on both sides. There would be no privacy here.

The petty officer smiled brightly. "Right straight down there bed number twenty-one A. Paul doesn't get many visitors. He'll be happy to see you."

Nick passed bed after bed and every one of them contained a young man with one or more of his limbs either in a cast or missing. Orthopedics was a large department. He could see Paul sitting in a chair and although his back was to him, he would know that black hair and profile anywhere. Another young man in a wheelchair sat opposite him. A blanket covered his lap but it was apparent that both legs were missing. They were playing cards on the bedside table they had pulled between them.

"Hey there, Paul." Nick kept his voice low so he would not startle him.

Paul turned and when he saw Nick his eyes brightened. "Nick!"

The two embraced and Nick spoke first. "How ya' doing?" He tried not to look at the thin left arm lying lifeless on his lap.

"Good, very good. I'm going home real soon."

"That *is* good. I'm on leave myself and heading for New York."

"New York? What in the hell's in New York?"

"Josie's there with her aunt and uncle and we have a baby boy."

"Man, I'm really happy for you. Let's go down to the sitting area so we can catch up." He touched his card-playing friend on the shoulder. "See you later."

Nick and Paul sat across from each other. Paul's face was still pale but worse was the sadness in his dark eyes. "I'm going home very shortly too. I don't know how I'll face Sam's wife and family. I was the one who talked him into enlisting."

"I'm sure he wouldn't have done it unless he wanted it himself."

"Maybe." Tears glazed Paul's eyes. "He was like a brother to me and I was proud of how well he did but this." His voice faltered.

Nick had never seen Paul show his emotions and it tore his heart. "I'm so sorry, Paul but he and his family knew the risks. You can't blame yourself."

"I try to tell myself that. Anyhow let's keep in touch. I want to hear about that boy of yours."

"You will I promise you. We'll see each other again I'll probably be reassigned after my leave."

The two men walked to the stairwell and shared a cigarette, talking of things only they would understand.

"Give me your address in Arizona and let me know if you decide to marry your girl."

Paul smiled. "It may take a while before I decide what is right and how I'll get by with this." He nodded briefly toward his useless arm.

"Just be sure and keep in touch and I'll send you a picture of little Danny."

They embraced tightly. Two thin gaunt friends brought together in the name of their country.

As he left the hospital Nick felt discouraged remembering the loss of his friends and comrades but he hoped that the heaviness in his heart would lighten when he finally saw Josie and his son.

Chapter XI
New York, 1945

The war in Europe was over! People were overjoyed that at least Hitler had been disposed of but the problem of Japan still loomed. It was rumored that a new kind of bomb was ready that would end the war completely. President Truman was very different from Roosevelt and many wondered if he was capable of making such important decisions as dropping the Atom Bomb. In the meantime many troops returned home and many more families faced the fact that a husband, father, son or brother would never be coming home.

Josie had not heard from Nick in such a long time that she felt he had probably forgotten her completely. She had sent him a letter when she moved to New York to be with her Aunt and Uncle but of course if he had not received it he would not even know where she was. She had written several times since then but had received no answer.

Josie watched from the doorway as Aunt Leah and Uncle Daniel played with the baby. A sliver of sun slanted across the babies golden curls and the soft cooing seemed on the verge of a giggle as Uncle Daniel blew on his tummy. Aunt Leah was smiling happily as the baby reached his chubby arms toward her. How sad it must have been for Aunt Leah to have never conceived a child. Josie remembered her aunt saying that she had been too old, a spinster really at thirty-six, to think of bearing a child. She had actually given up marrying until she met the handsome engineer recently returned from a stint in Puerto Rico. They met at a party given by Aunt Leah's friend. More than one young lady set her sights on him but he was tired of all the pretty faces he had met overseas and saw something deeper in the mature woman with the green eyes and pale freckles. He had been married once and fathered a child but in those days few men retained other than a monetary relationship with the child of a failed marriage. It mattered little to Leah who had at last met the person she had waited for all her life. They made a perfect couple and in Josie's life of seeing her own parents bitter marriage it was what she dreamed of with her own husband.

They had given her a home when she needed it most of all and now she had given them the pleasure of a "grandchild." Josie had decided to name the baby after her uncle as an honor of sorts for taking her in at such a crucial time or there might have been no baby at all. The powers that be would have whisked him away to never be seen again. Instead here was Daniel Joseph Romano. Josie had put Nick's name on the birth certificate as the father even though she had worried if it was legal. Uncle Daniel said it would make it much easier in the long run.

"He's such a good baby!" Aunt Leah said.

"A happy well-fed baby is a good baby." Uncle Daniel said proudly.

"Speaking of that," Josie picked up the baby. "The well is overflowing and this little guy has to eat."

"Look, this is what you've been waiting for." Aunt Leah held out a fat envelope.

Josie's heart raced as she took the envelope and read the return address.

Tears welled in her eyes. "Oh my God, what if...... ?"

"What if nothing. Read it my dear. That's the only way you're going to know what it says."

Josie smiled and tore it open with trembling fingers. There were a lot of pages and the Marine Corp Logo at the top of each one. Josie sank into the chair and began to read.

My dearest one,

I have read all your letters one by one and I am so sorry for all you went through. If only I could have been there to help. The last letter is by far the best news I have ever had. A boy! Thank you my darling and please thank your aunt and uncle for me. Danny is one of my favorite names and thank you for adding my father's name, Joseph. He would be very proud of that and my mother will be too. I have written her and told her about the baby and she is anxious to meet you both. I let her believe that we married before I left. She is rather old fashioned about things like that and though I didn't exactly lie, I just let her believe what she assumed. I don't know how you managed without money but I swear I will pay your aunt and uncle back. I want to tell you about my experiences but first I must tell you that James is dead. Of the two Indians we were assigned to guard one is also dead and the other in the hospital. I seem to be the only one unscathed. I know my mother prayed very hard for me and I hope in some way to make my life worthy. I know I have changed and I feel it's for the better. I hope you will still want me and that we can make a life together. I am coming to New York on leave and hope to get out of the Marines as soon as the Japanese surrender. I will arrive one week from the date of this letter. All my love to you and Danny, and my regards to your aunt and uncle. Nick

"Aunt Leah, he's coming here!" Josie hugged her aunt.

Josie checked the date on the letter. "That's tomorrow. We'd better get ready!"

Her aunt nodded, "I think you've been ready for a very long time."

That night sleep refused to come to Josie's cluttered mind. It was filled with doubts and questions and yet an undeniable joy to see once again this man who had captured her heart. How many times had she dreamed of making love until the ache in her groin became unbearable and she reached down and gently massaged until the familiar feeling washed over her. When she first began to nurse Danny she was ashamed of the erotic feelings his suckling brought back to her body. Finally it had become a routine but how would it feel to be with Nick again. She climbed out of bed and glanced at the crib where Danny lay sleeping without a care. She smiled at the tousled curls so like his fathers. What would Nick think of this little image of himself? She went to the window and looked at the stars barely visible between the buildings and thought of the wide-open sky at home in Michigan. Stars by the millions crowded the space above the shining black water and the bright silver moon throwing her beams to light the way for dreams to climb the stairway to the stars. She would never want to live in a place like this. They didn't even have houses here they were just buildings divided into "flats". She wondered where the name came from. One flat on top of another probably. Some buildings had four flats and some even more. Josie tried to picture Colorado but of course she could not. She knew from geography that the mountains were very high and they certainly didn't have a Great Lake but they did have streams that flowed down the mountainsides. She wondered what it was like where Nick grew up and his mother still lived. She was getting ahead of herself for sure. Maybe Nick wouldn't want to get married and take her with him. He said he had changed and she had too. Having a baby changed a good deal of things. One thing Josie knew was that tomorrow would be one of the most important days of her life.

"How will he know how to find us?" Josie asked.

Uncle Dan took a sip of coffee. "He'll just tell the cabdriver the address and *veroom* he'll be here."

Josie laughed at her uncle's casual answer. She knew he was right.

The day seemed to drag on. "Telephone!" Aunt Leah sounded excited.

"Hello."

"Josie, I just got in. They tell me it's quite a way to your address so I'll be there in about an hour okay?"

"Yes, okay, I'll see you then." The phone clicked. "Oh Aunt Leah he'll be here in an hour."

"Good. Let's get that dinner started. He'll be starved. This will be his first home cooked meal, so let's make it fabulous."

Tears welled in Josie's eyes as she gave her aunt a quick hug. What would she do without her?

The doorbell rang and for a moment everything stood still then her aunt nodded toward the door and Josie jumped up leaving Danny in the highchair, his face covered with applesauce. She opened the door and there stood a very thin Marine in a drab uniform. He dropped his bag on the porch and took off his cap and there was the Nick she remembered as he took her in his arms. He covered her face with kisses and their tears mingled as they clung together.

"Come in, come in you two. I'm Dan and this is my wife Leah. Welcome to our home."

"Thank you sir." The men shook hands and Nick bent to kiss Aunt Leah.

"I've heard wonderful things about you." Aunt Leah blushed and smiled. The smell of roast beef and garlic and apple pie drifted from the kitchen. "There's someone else who wants to meet you."

Nick followed her and saw Danny waving his spoon in indignation at being left in the middle of his meal. Nick swept him up applesauce and all and kissed him and held him so tightly he squirmed to get loose. Josie took him and wiped his face. Thank you God, she breathed as her heart threatened to burst with happiness. At long last she had a real family.

They were alone at last. Nick and Josie sat on the edge of the bed kissing gently, removing each other's clothes, piece by piece.

"I've got stretch marks." Josie's voice was a low whisper to keep from waking Danny. "Neither of us knew you were supposed to put cocoa butter on your tummy until it was too late."

Nick bent his head to kiss the pink marks that ran like tiny trails across her stomach. "You went through so much alone."

"But you saw destruction and killing and lost your best friend."

"Let's forget all that now. I love you so much." It was as though they had never been apart. Nick kissed her breasts heavy with milk, probed her mouth with his tongue and she responded. They explored every inch of their bodies and when they climaxed together the ecstasy was complete and they fell into a deep sleep.

Nick slid out of bed trying not to wake Josie. He looked at her lying with her hair like a golden halo on the pillow. He knew she had nursed the baby in the wee hours of the morning but he had pretended to be asleep. His emotions were stretched to the breaking point and he didn't trust himself to watch her nurse Danny. He walked outside in the cool dawn. Josie was right. You had to look straight up to see the sky. The stars were beginning to fade. Nick lit a cigarette and leaned against the wall. He had decided to ask Josie to marry him today so that when he was discharged he could take her home as his wife. His plans to go back to school could be put on hold and he was sure he could get his old job back.

It was time he took responsibility. He stubbed out his cigarette and went back to the bedroom.

"Did you sleep all right?" Josie stretched and held out her arms to him.

It was nearly an hour later when Danny let them know he was ready for his breakfast.

The next few days were perfect. Uncle Dan arranged for them to be married in his old friend Judge Taylor's chambers with her aunt and uncle as witnesses and Danny cooing in Aunt Leah's arms. Nick wore his uniform and Josie wore a simple blue dress enhanced by a corsage of pink rosebuds and babies breath. There was no music and the elegant office smelled of leather but nothing mattered to Josie and Nick except the words that would make them man and wife.

Do you Dominic Anthony Romano take Josephine Ann Mofford to be your wedded wife to have and to hold in sickness and in health as long as you both shall live?

"I do."

Nick sipped the thin gold band on her finger next to the tiny diamond he had given her so long ago.

The judge repeated the vow for Josie who slipped a gold band on Nick's finger that Uncle Dan had given her, saying only that it was one he had in a box for a long time.

"By the power invested to me by the state of New York I now pronounce you husband and wife. May God bless you both." Nick bent his head and kissed Josie and for a moment it was as though they were the only two people in the world. Then suddenly Danny let out a cry that seemed to say, Hey don't forget about me. Everyone laughed and hugged one another.

They celebrated by going to dinner and dancing at the VFW where Uncle Dan was a member. They took turns holding

Danny who seemed very content to attend the celebration of his parents.

Nick was restless and Josie noticed that he spent a lot of time on the porch seemingly brooding and smoking. She had never known him to smoke while they were in Michigan and one day while holding Danny an ash dropped from his cigarette and landed on Danny's sweater. Nick brushed it off but not before it made a tiny hole in the blue knit.

"I wish you wouldn't smoke while carrying Danny." Josie had not meant for her voice to be so sharp but Nick reacted quickly and handed the baby to her at once. "I'm sorry Nick, but it just seems like you smoke so much anymore."

"Have you thought that maybe that's all I have to do here?"

"I thought you were happy here."

"That's not the point. There are things I have to do. I really must leave."

Josie nodded dreading the time he would leave but savoring the time they had spent together.

Just then Uncle Dan burst into the room. "Excuse me but this couldn't wait. The war is all but over! The Enola Gay has just dropped the largest bomb of all on Hiroshima. Much bigger than the one a few days ago dropped on Nagasaki."

Nick seemed stunned. "Those poor people. Thousands will be killed. Women and children too. It's a horrible death you know. They'll be torn apart and burned and mutilated."

Uncle Dan was surprised at Nick's reaction. "They were the enemy son, they killed and tortured thousands of our boys. This is a time for celebration."

"I know but women and children, the elderly. It's hell."

Nick was right. It was hell. Newsreels from Japan showed the devastation and the horror of the living. Lines of ash covered people like ants carrying their belongings in a small bundle wandered about searching for relatives and someplace to go. Uncle Dan was right too. The Japanese surrendered and the war was over.

Chapter XII
Colorado

The streets of New York were a mass of humanity. Screaming, laughing, crying and flag-waving people pushed and shoved their way toward Times Square to celebrate the end of the war. Taxi's moved at a snails pace and Nick worried that they would miss their train. Uncle Daniel had called in favors, made phone calls and finally secured a compartment for Nick, Josie and baby Danny on the streamliner from New York to Denver, Colorado. Now that the war was over Nick would return to duty only to be released as soon as the paperwork could be completed, but in the meantime he would finish his leave in Colorado. They decided that Josie would accompany him on his return to Colorado to meet his mother and family. Josie's aunt and uncle would be leaving New York and returning to their home in Michigan since that had been a temporary assignment for the duration. They would miss Josie and the baby beyond belief and could only hope that they could stay close. Even as the war had changed so many things, now the aftermath would continue to change the lives of many.

The train was packed with soldiers and families, some even standing in the aisles. Josie held Danny tightly as they made their way to the compartment. A large bulky soldier with stripes the entire length of his sleeve was pushed against her.

"Sorry Mam," the soldier apologized, "cute little girl ya' got there. What's her name?"

"*His* name is Danny."

"Guess the curls fooled me." The soldier laughed as he moved on.

Nick closed the door of the compartment. "Thank God for privacy. I don't think I could ride all the way to Denver in coach. Looks like Danny gets a haircut as soon as possible, that smart-ass soldier calling him a girl."

"Oh Nick, he's only a baby. Why do you take everything so seriously?"

Nick leaned back and lit a cigarette and did not answer. Josie had a feeling this was going to be a very long ride.

Anna and her husband Tony herded them toward an older Chevy stowing the luggage in the trunk. Nick had not seen Anna since her marriage to one of the guys from the old neighborhood and as they kissed she seemed almost like a stranger. She hugged Josie and took Danny in her arms.

"Oh, Nicky what a wonderful family!" Anna settled Josie and Danny in the back seat and joined them. "We're going to get acquainted. Mama will be so happy to see you."

The little house in the coal-mining town where Nick grew up looked especially small and drab under the cloudy sky. The town itself looked small and drab too, Nick thought as he noticed the mines looked quiet and deserted.

Tony noticed Nick's observation, "The mines dried up around here. The coal wasn't the right kind and most of the men went to war or to work in the factories."

Nick nodded. "So I see."

They pulled up in front of the house and the curtain in the living room moved as Mama dropped it and burst through the door.

Nick enveloped his mother in his arms. She felt smaller than he remembered and smelled of soap and garlic. Tears rolled down Nick's cheeks and she pulled his face down to hers kissing him soundly. "You come home safe, thanks to the Holy

Mother." She turned to Josie and the baby and drew them into her arms. "Welcome home!"

It was a festive occasion and the family gathered around the table. Mama asked Nick to say grace and strange as it felt his memory of the family prayer came to him, choked him with its simple message and when he finished and they all said "Amen" and made the sign of the cross, Nick felt he had truly come home.

Mama brought in a steaming pot of potato and spinach soup followed by a platter of chicken simmered in tomato, garlic, oregano, onion and wild mushrooms. Homemade pasta in olive oil and garlic sprinkled with parmesan cheese and thick crusty bread hot and fragrant from the oven. The wine was robust and deep garnet in color, and when they finally pushed away their plates Mama brought in coffee and brandy, tiny almond cookies and fresh fruit. Tony produced two cigars from his breast pocket and handed one to Nick and the men took their brandy and went to the porch to smoke.

They sat in silence and Tony was first to speak. "So what do you think you'll do now?"

Nick shook his head. "First I've got to find a place to live then find a job and I'll need a car. I never thought I'd have a family to worry about."

"Why not leave Josie and the baby with Mama and come back to Denver with Anna and me? You have to be mustered out from there anyhow. We'd put the family up but all we have is a bed on the back porch."

"Thanks, I'll stay here for now but I do have to be in Denver to look for a job so I may take you up on it."

Nick had been a civilian for over two months and Josie and Danny were still at his mothers and he was bunking on Anna's porch. It was not what Nick had envisioned but he tried not to be discouraged.

"I have covered every place I can think of but it just seems like I don't have the right skills." Nick was sitting at the table with Anna and got up to pour another cup of coffee.

"Have you gone to see Mr. Kolinski?" Anna's dark eyes were sympathetic.

"Not yet. I just kept hoping for something better. You know Anna I never thought that when I came home I'd have to worry about a family."

A smile crept across Anna's face. "It's a very nice family Nick. It'll work out."

"I suppose. Well I'm off." Nick rose and stubbed out his cigarette.

Mr. Kolinski's service station looked quiet and run-down as Nick approached. It was a shame Nick thought. Such a great location, only two blocks from the state capitol and near Colfax Avenue that ran east and west through the whole city. It should be booming. Across the street on the other side of Colfax Nick saw a brand new sign rising above a modern station proclaiming not only gas but cigarettes, drinks and snacks. Nick shook his head. His old boss had let progress pass him by.

The driveway was empty but there was sound of movement in the garage and Nick called out. "Hey, anybody here?"

Mr. Kolinski rolled out from under a car and looked up to see Nick. His lined face broke into a smile. "Nick! Oh my boy, how are you?"

"Fine, sir and you?"

They embraced awkwardly, Mr. Kolinski conscious of the grease on his clothes and hands.

"I've been wondering when you'd get back." He wiped his hands on the red rag he pulled from his pocket. "Let's go in the office where we can talk."

The office was cramped and cluttered and the coffee on the hot plate was black and steaming. Mr. Kolinski poured it into two mugs and pushed some papers off the chair and motioned Nick to sit. He sat behind the desk. "I been hopin' you'd want your old job back."

Nick heard the warmth and eagerness in the old man's voice. "Thing is, I got a family now, a wife and boy. I need a job with a future."

"You got it boy! I'll make you a partner. You're good with figures. I'll let you do the figurin' but after expenses we'll split what's left. How about it?"

Nick was stunned. Images rushed through his mind. No hourly wage. The harder he worked, the more he'd make. He'd turn the place around. Excitement flowed through his veins. He stood up and leaned across the desk holding out his hand. "You've got yourself a deal."

Mr. Kolinski grasped Nick's hand and his wrinkled face beamed. "Welcome partner. Here's to a new beginning!"

Chapter XIII
The Reservation

The Greyhound Bus was filled with Indians who worked in the towns surrounding the reservation and Paul in his Marine Corp uniform looked as out of place with his own kind as he had felt so many times among the white man. The locals regarded him as a stranger and their sardonic looks made him wish he had bought some clothes and changed before catching the bus. He had changed from the train to the bus in Flagstaff and in his haste to get home it had not occurred to him that the war had little effect on the remote desert of Arizona. Many of the passengers dismounted at Window Rock that was the center of the Navajo Nation, and except for an elderly man he found himself alone. His thoughts whirled in his mind and his useless arm lay in his lap.

The old man turned in his seat. "You live on the reservation or just visitin?"

" I live there I guess, for now at least. My mother and girlfriend live there."

"Most of the youngins' live in Window Rock now. The government built some cinderblock houses that look like the white man's houses. Got 'lectricity and such."

Paul shook his head. "I didn't know that. I've been gone about four years."

"Last stop." The bus driver's voice cut in.

Paul could see the old general store in the distance and the hogans looked mostly deserted. Apparently the old man had been right and the younger people lived in the housing the government had built. It was all a part of the reservation but it seemed that it was divided into the new and the old. Paul hopped out of the bus, saluted the old man and started off in the direction of his mother's hogan. As he approached he could see his mother weaving a colorful rug just as in the old days and a lump rose in his throat. She sensed his presence and rose from her work and held out her arms.

Paul was not used to sleeping on the ground and slept fitfully turning around in his mind the options and obligations of his life. One obligation was to see Sam's family and the other was to go to Morning Star and ask her to marry him. He had very little contact with her over the years but he knew in his heart she would be waiting.

Sam's family was well and had adjusted to the fact that Sam would not return. The boys had grown strong and healthy and their grandfather was an intricate part of their life. Sam's wife laid her hands over his and assured him that Sam would have enlisted even without his example. Paul felt the burden of guilt lift from his shoulders. "If I can do anything for you just get in touch."

"Thank you. I want to make sure the boys get a good education. Are you still planning to teach?"

"Yes, I'll finish getting my degree. Good-bye for now." Paul turned feeling happier than he had in a long time.

Morning Star sat cross-legged on a blanket surrounded by bowls of many shapes and sizes. She was getting them ready for sale at the Center in Window Rock. She looked up to see Paul striding toward her his feet making clouds of red dust. She rose to greet him and as he encircled her with his arm she was conscious of the arm that hung limply at his side. She lifted her face to his and he kissed her deeply savoring the scent of her hair and the smoothness of her cheek against his.

Finally they parted and she pulled him inside where it was cool and brought him a drink and cornbread. "We have much to discuss." He said softly and she smiled in agreement.

Morning Star and Paul were married five days later in a traditional Navajo ceremony. Paul had explained to her that he would be going back to the University in the fall and she had begged him to let her stay on the reservation and they would be together on weekends. Paul was aware that the country had changed since the war and he realized that he too had changed. Could he blend back into the culture of his ancestors? For the first time he was afraid for their marriage and their future.

Chapter XIV
New Beginning

Josie was beginning to understand what it meant to be a wife and mother. She had lived with her aunt and uncle during the birth of her son and his subsequent care. She now realized it was very different when there was only one of you to do the cooking, cleaning and laundry in addition to the care of a child. She also realized that she had no conception of what it meant to have a husband. Playing at marriage as they had done in Michigan had scarcely prepared her for the real thing. It seemed to Josie that Nick was never home to share in the care of Danny or even spend any time with her. He had taken his job at the station so intensely serious that Josie was of the opinion that Mr. Kolinski saw more of him than she did. Nick had tried to explain that he was trying to build up the business so that he would make more money.

As though all that were not enough Nick had also enrolled in the local college to study business and accounting so to better run the station. The G.I.Bill helped to pay for college but it was all time consuming.

This particular evening was not a school night so Josie had prepared a dinner of pot roast and vegetables and looked forward to Nick's enjoyment of the food and a chance to sit quietly and tell her about his day. When he had not arrived by seven, she put Danny to bed and dinner back in the oven. She was pregnant again and tired by evening. Disappointed she picked up the book she had been reading and curled up in a chair. Josie was startled when she heard the clock strike nine and realized she had dozed and that Nick still had not come home. She stretched her legs and arms and heard Nick's key in the lock.

"Where have you been?" Josie's voice was sharp.

"At the station, where else would I be? I've been going over the books and they sure need going over. They're a mess."

"I just thought we could have a decent dinner together." Josie's voice trailed away.

"I'm sorry darling, truly I am. Come sit with me while I fix a plate." Nick pulled her to her feet and kissed her. His charm never failed she thought.

"I've got great news." Nick said between mouthfuls of food. "Mr. Kolinski is thinking of going to California to live with his daughter and wants me to buy the place."

"But we have no money."

"He says I can pay him every month and he'll hold the papers until it's paid."

"Doesn't he need more money than that?"

"He's going to sell his house. The payment on the station will just be income. It's a great opportunity and I can do what I want. I have lots of ideas to boost business." Nick's eyes sparkled as he talked and his hands gestured.

Josie knew this was what Nick wanted. He'd be his own boss. She picked up the dishes and put them in the sink. Nick followed and put his arms around her and nuzzled her neck and patted her stomach.

"It'll be great and we'll need more money now with another mouth to feed." He picked her up in his arms and carried her to bed.

Chapter XV
1955
The Navajo Reservation

Paul looked up from the papers he was correcting at the young man standing before him and smiled. "Joe Running Horse, how are you?"

"I'm good." He dipped his head shyly. He was dressed in the typical dress of the white schoolboy. "I came by today to see if you would attend my graduation next week?"

Paul came around the desk and put his arm around the boy's shoulder. "Of course I'll come. I'm really proud of you and I know your father would be too. Your Mother told me you graduated with honors and plan to go on to college."

"Yes Sir, I'm already accepted at the University in Flagstaff. My mother told me to invite you to dinner tonight. Can you come?"

"I'll be happy to get one of your Mother's delicious dinners and we can have a nice visit."

The boy grinned and waved, "See you later!"

Paul turned back to his desk. How time flies. Sam's son had been seven when the war was over and his father had not come home. He had been a stoic young boy but Paul had seen the grief in his eyes. His grandfather had shown not grief but anger and that had worried Paul. He didn't want the boy to grow up hating the white men whose war they fought. It was their war too but the older generation did not want to accept that. They wanted to stay on the reservation and keep their own way of life. The old man wanted young Joe to take over the sheep and help his mother. There were two other children to think about and they were growing up too. Paul had convinced them that Joe must have an education. The world was changing he told the old man and they could not live completely a part from the white man. Paul had come back to teach for that very reason. Joe had come to school and Paul had seen the potential that lay behind the solemn dark eyes. Now he wanted to be a doctor and start a clinic on the reservation. The way of the shaman was past even though many still believed in them. Paul convinced the old man that Joe must go on with his education.

Paul closed his eyes and could see Morning Star as she lay on the blanket in their hogan as her labor progressed. Paul had sensed there was trouble when the women of the tribe called in the medicine man not normally used for births. He had wanted to put her in his pickup and take her to Flagstaff but the women had shooed him out and he had let them have their way. When the baby came out at last there was no cry, no breath. The infant had strangled by his own cord. Paul pushed the women aside and knelt beside Morning Star. Her eyes opened slightly as she felt his cheek against hers. She mouthed the word baby but no sound came. Her eyes closed. He remembered his strangled cry as he held her and saw the pool of blood beneath her. He cursed his useless arm that could not cradle her and shouted at the women who had stopped him at the door. "Damn you! I wanted to take her to Flagstaff!" He saw the Shaman with his beads and herbs and the midwife whose face was stoic as she removed the baby from his wife's chest and began to clean her.

"It was meant to be." Her voice was low.

"No, how do you know that?" Paul shouted. "They have many new ways now. She could have been saved!" His glance scoured the room. He clenched his fists. I hate them, all of them. I hate their traditions and ignorance. He stalked out to his truck and climbed in. He lay his head against the steering column and sobbed.

The funeral was held the next day and Paul's grief and fury were at war in his heart. As soon as the funeral was over Paul said good-bye to his mother, packed a duffel bag, threw his meager belongings into the pick-up and left for the University. Even now many years later sweat poured down his face mingled with tears and he felt the helpless frustration of that day. Yes, they needed a clinic with a real doctor who would have cut her open and saved them both. Paul gathered up his papers and closed the school door behind him.

That evening Paul walked the short distance to the hogan that had been enlarged while Sam was still alive to accommodate his father and their children but still contained the symbols of the old life. They still slept on the floor and the meals were cooked on the open fire in the center of the room and the smoke rose and curled toward the sky. It was early June and still cool in the evening hours. The cacti were in bloom, dark pink and yellow and blue lupine crawled along the ground under his feet. The sun was turning from orange to cardinal and the shadows on the rocks and arroyos were a rosy hue. Paul paused to remember how Sam had come to him that evening so much like this, to tell him he would join him in the Marine Corp. Paul shook his head to dispel the memories of another time and another life.

This was a new day and Sam's son was to graduate from high school and begin a world that would take on what the white man had to offer to bring their people out of the dark age of ignorance.

Chapter XV
Colorado, 1960

Josie turned the "56 Chevy" into the driveway. "Okay everybody out. Get started on your homework and Mary Beth you set the table."

The three boys had come within two years of one another and then at last five years later the girl she had prayed for. They piled out of the car, the boys wrestling and punching one another and Mary Beth giggling at their antics. Josie loved her little brood but she had made up her mind that this was quite enough. It seemed to her that she had been pregnant forever and just last month she had been afraid it had happened again. It'd be just my luck to get pregnant when the children are at an age when they can take care of themselves. Danny was a senior in high school, David a sophomore and Jerard just finishing the Catholic prep school. Mary Beth was a very independent ten - year old. Josie knew many women who had babies when their oldest was in high school and she did not want to be one of them. She had been relieved when her scare proved to be just a little glitch in timing and when she was sure that she was safe, she made an appointment with her doctor and told him she wanted the safest thing he had to keep her from getting pregnant. "I don't believe in abortion, but see nothing wrong in prevention."

He knew she was Catholic and supressed a smile as he faced her across the desk.

"So you're afraid to trust the rhythm method?"

"Yes, Dr. Foley. I love my children but enough is enough."

"Then I would suggest that we measure you for a diaphragm. It's about 99% sure."

"You know, I'm actually not a Catholic. I never joined the church officially. I was never certain about things like birth control being wrong."

"I couldn't agree more, so go with the nurse and she'll measure and explain about the gel to use with it. Good luck."

Josie brought her thoughts back to the moment and thought how much more relaxed she was now that she didn't have to worry about getting pregnant. So then why hadn't she told Nick about it? Would he feel it was an act against the church or against him? He had never pushed her to join the church. It was enough for him that she quit going to her Protestant church and went with him instead. All the children had been baptized and had gone to parochial schools so no one ever questioned her about not receiving communion. She doubted they even noticed. Anyway she had decided that tonight she would have a nice dinner, send the children to bed, then fix Nick his favorite drink, snuggle up so he'd know she wanted him and then she'd tell him her little secret. She hoped that he would be pleased and carry her up to bed.

Nick did not come home for dinner.

Josie was a light sleeper, as are most mothers and she heard the sound of Nick's key in the lock. She glanced at the bedside clock that was just approaching three AM. She turned toward the wall feigning sleep as the footfalls reached the top of the stairs and came into the room. A gasp and soft curse told her Nick had hit his toe on the foot of the bed. She could hear the stream hit the water as he urinated but he did not flush obviously thinking it might awaken her. She breathed evenly as he slid into bed beside her and the odor of whiskey and cigarettes filled her nostrils. He was soon snoring softly but Josie lay awake. She could not help but wonder if he was seeing another woman or if it was truly just "some of the guys" as he so often put it when he was absent or late. He had done so well in business and was more than generous with her and the children. He had started with just a service station and built it into a small empire. He had a large garage, a beautiful restaurant, a store that sold snacks and groceries, even cosmetics. He had bought land surrounding the original station that still had old houses of disrepair such as Mrs. O'Grady's where Nick had roomed, and Mr. Kolinski's that had been sold once and gone into foreclosure. He had torn them all down and borrowed money to put up the new buildings.

Nick was a dedicated and hard worker and the business was very successful. The whole family was proud of him. Nick had one serious flaw and that was to hire old buddies from the town where he grew up. Most of them seemed to take advantage of him and tried to turn the growing business into a "good ole' boys club." After business hours they organized illegal card games playing for money. Nick had always been conscientious but his drinking and carousing with his old friends sometimes interfered with his good judgment.

"Good morning, sleepyhead." Nick was already showered, shaved and looking dapper in a soft brown suit, white shirt and tan striped tie.

"Good morning. You missed dinner."

"Sorry, darling, some of the guys got together and we talked business for hours." Nick bent and kissed her. He smelled of toothpaste and cologne and his hair was perfect. "Have a good day and I'll try to get home early tonight."

"Do you want some coffee?"

"No, Susie makes it at the office. See you tonight." He rushed down the stairs and was gone.

Josie went into the bathroom and removed the unused diaphragm. She locked the door and stood looking at her body as she ran a bath. I scarcely look like a twenty-year old but not bad for a mother of four the oldest nearly out of high school. She slid into the warm water. What was happening to them?

Danny banged on the door. "Hey, Mom where's my baseball uniform?"

Her day had begun.

The day was approaching for Mama Romano's eightieth birthday and Nick had decided to give a big party in his restaurant to surprise her. It wouldn't be as grand as the Brown Palace but he knew she would think it was wonderful. He decided to close the restaurant that night and make it a real occasion. He would leave the invitations up to Josie and his sister Anna and told her to invite all the friends and relatives from Louisville.

Josie and Anna made a date for lunch to make plans and Josie told Anna she would pick her up. They decided to go to an Italian place in Louisville where they might get an inspiration for the party. As they sat across from each other Josie said quietly, "Anna do you think I'm starting to look old and dull?"

Anna laughed and then realized that Josie was serious. " I think you look darn good. You're always dressed nice, your hair always done and you're still slim. What more would you want?"

Josie shook her head, "I don't know. It's just that Nick doesn't seem as interested anymore."

Anna took Josie's hand. "Nick wants the world for all of you. That's why he works so hard. He wants all the boys to have not just a college education but a real profession. He wants them to have everything he didn't. That doesn't mean he's not interested in you."

They gave their order to the waiter who said, "Aren't you Nick's sister?"

Anna nodded. "Boy, he sure has got it made. Tell him Sharky said Hi."

Anna shrugged. "See what I mean? Local boy makes good."

Josie smiled. "It seems so strange to me that Nick never talks about your father. When I ask about him, he just says he died young from an aneurysm Do they know what caused it? It doesn't seem natural."

"You honestly don't know? Papa was an alcoholic and had what they now call bi-polar syndrome. Then they just called it "crazy" and put them in mental institutions. They were awful places with severely retarded people mixed with those who were criminally insane and people like Papa. They gave him shock treatments but all that did was make him listless. Nick never seemed to understand why they were able to get away with it. Of course Mama didn't have any resources and our uncle thought it was the right thing to do. Nick was deeply hurt by the gossip and stigma. He's never gotten over it."

Josie felt tears spring to her eyes." Poor Nick he has carried this with him all his life."

"Hey, we've got a party to plan." Anna pulled out a notebook and began to write.

The party was a tremendous success. They managed to keep it a secret from Mama and when she and Gina pulled up in front of the restaurant in the car Nick had sent for them, Mama looked at the red neon sign spread across the entrance. "Dominic's" the sign seemed to shout and underneath in smaller letters, "Italian Cusine."

As they entered the restaurant Mama was stunned to see so many guests and the opulence of the decorations. It seemed that all the people she had ever known were gathered here to celebrate her birthday. She looked up at her handsome son and touched his lips lightly, her eyes full of tears. "Thank you," she murmured holding his arm as he led her to the head table.

Nick was in his glory. He never enjoyed anything as much as pleasing his family and he went from table to table greeting old friends and welcoming new ones from among the customers and politicians across the street in the state capitol. . It was a diversified group in economics and age. His mother's old friends from the days of the coal mining mingled with their children, young people and affluent men and women of the day's society.

Josie felt exhaustion and relief as she prepared for bed. It had gone well, Thank God, she thought. She had her doubts about the guest list but as usual Nick seemed unerringly correct. He sat on the edge of the bed still too excited to sleep.

He had invited Paul to come from Arizona and had asked him to stay here at the house. He was a neat and quiet guest, his dark eyes taking in everything in this world so far removed from the reservation. He was a teacher and devoted his life to preparing the young native men to take their place in modern society.

"I'm going to check on Paul and see if he needs anything." Nick took Josies face between his hands and kissed her gently on the lips. "Thank you for all you did to make tonight special."

Josie,s lips were warm and inviting but he rose from the bed and closed the door quietly behind him. He tapped lightly on the guest room door.

"It's so great to have you here." Nick said "Would you care for a drink or snack?"

Paul smiled and patted his stomach. "I've eaten more tonight than I usually eat in a week. Your mother sure enjoyed the party."

"Yes, she's a great old gal. Has always been behind me all the way."

"You're lucky to have your mother and a wonderful wife too."

"How come you never remarried? It's been a long time."

"I don't know. I'm so busy and now I'm working on getting a hospital built."

Nick shook his head "All work and well, you know what they say. It's not good."

Paul grinned. "I've never met anyone either. That could be part of it."

"Aw, there must be some pretty squaws up there."

A flush darkened Paul's brown skin. "Maybe that's the problem. I'm not sure what I want in a women. In some ways I'm too Americanized and yet what white woman would want to live on a reservation?"

Nick had never thought of that complication. He felt empathy for his good friend. "You'll find someone one of these days. Thanks for coming. Good night."

Nick slid into bed. As he turned out the light he glanced at Josie's face. Her honey colored hair lay spread on the pillow, her face peaceful, her hand tucked under her chin. He kissed her and she nuzzled close and he held her tight. I am lucky he thought. What must it be like to be alone?

The next morning Nick was up, showered and dressed when Josie opened her eyes. "Leaving already?"

"Yes, I've a million things to do. Will you tell Paul good-bye for me?"

"Of course. I'll make him some breakfast. I wish you'd wait and eat too."

"No can do, doll. I have an appointment with a District Judge and I can't keep him waiting."

"What about?"

" I asked him the same question. He said it was some personal business. You don't keep a judge waiting."

Nick took Josie in his arms and let his hands wander inside her gown. Her skin was soft and he could feel his manhood beginning to harden. He stopped, gave her a quick kiss and ran down the steps.

Josie had just made a pot of coffee when Paul came into the kitchen. He was carrying a small canvas bag with a garment bag over his shoulder.

"Good morning." Josie grabbed the bag from him. "I just made a fresh pot of coffee and some muffins and fruit, so we'll just put these things in the hall and you'll sit down, ok?"

"Thank you, I'd be honored." Paul ducked his head slightly and smiled.

As they finished their second cup of coffee, Josie said, "Now tell me about this hospital you want to get started."

Paul looked at her in surprise. "I didn't think you'd be interested. I can't seem to get the women themselves interested."

"Maybe they don't know how to go about letting you know."

"I put up a notice in the community center and got no response at all."

"Paul, I have to admit I've never had any contact with a reservation or with Indian women but from things I've read I think they probably need to be educated about what a clinic would mean to them. You say how you are teaching the young men about the outside world but what about the women?"

Paul met her blue eyes with his and she could see the admiration in them. "You're right. I need a woman to give them some classes. Most of the girls know nothing of modern contraception or if they do get pregnant, of pre-natal care. Mostly they just want to get away from the reservation and that leads to sex and drugs just like it does in the men."

Josie shook her head. "It's so sad but of course it happens in many cultures, not just on reservations."

"True."

"I must tell you something, Paul. Since the boys have gone away to school, I became sort of bored and I have been taking classes at the college in nursing and I really like it. There is a lot of psychology involved and I find it fascinating."

"Nick never mentioned it."

Josie leaned forward gazing into those deep dark eyes. "Nick ignores it, so I've quit talking about it. Anyhow, I'll speak to my professor and she may have some ideas for getting someone up there to help you."

"Thanks for your interest but I doubt Colorado could get involved in Arizona."

"I don't see why not. The Federal Government has a committee on Indian affairs and that includes all states."

"You're a smart lady, Mrs. Romano."

"Please don't call me that. You and Nick have been friends for years. Why have you never called me by my first name?"

Josie saw the blush begin under the dark brown of his skin and her heart was filled with compassion for this dear friend who had never felt comfortable calling her by name because of his race. She laid her hand on his arm. "My name is Josephine." Somehow Josie didn't seem appropriate for this new friendship.

Chapter XVI

It was a typical spring day as Josie walked across the campus toward the parking lot. Trees were bursting with new green leaves and the flowering plum trees bent under their purple blossoms. A gentle breeze tugged at her hair and students with backpacks filled the sidewalks. Josie's exams were over and she would graduate with honors among the class that were primarily the age of her children. She was proud that she had made it and made a mental list of the things she had to do. Friday night was Mary Beth's prom and she had promised to pick up her dress at the alterations department of Macys. The boys would be coming home from their respective colleges so she had better have plenty of food on hand.

As she drove into the garage an hour later Josie was surprised to see Nick's car already there. She removed the prom dress carefully, grabbing a bag of groceries with the other hand. She pushed open the door and saw Nick sitting at the kitchen table a half-empty bottle of Jack Daniels and a glass of the amber brew in his hand.

"Hi" Josie said brightly, "Can you give me a hand?"

Nick rose slowly and went to bring in the groceries. As he set them on the counter he turned to Josie. "We have to talk." He said quietly.

Josie realized that something was very wrong. All the joy of the day drained from her body. "What is it?"

"Sit down." Nick's voice was weary. "I have bad news. I've tried to tell you but now I have no choice. The county is taking my business, all of it."

"What do you mean? They can't do that."

"It seems they can. The county is building a new complex next to the capitol and they need my property. Oh, they're going to pay for it but they will tear down everything to build the new building." Nick's voice broke and tears filled his eyes. "All the work I've put into it all these years will be gone."

Josie put her arms around him and held him as though he were an injured child.

"We'll take the money and start over."

Nick shook his head. "It won't work. I've borrowed too much and they won't pay that kind of money. We'll be lucky if we can keep this house." He buried his head in his hands and his shoulders shook as he tried to get control.

"Darling it will work out. I know it."

Nick raised his head. He was relieved that it was finally out in the open with Josie, but the boys would be home soon. How could he possibly tell them?

The days seemed to fly by. Josie's graduation and subsequent "pinning" when the nurses received their cap and pin was a time of pride and happiness for her even with Nick's business woes hanging over their head.

Mary Beth attended her prom looking very beautiful and grown up. Her escort was a boy they knew, a good student, polite and acceptable. The boys came home from college with plans for the summer mostly work-related and still nothing was said about the problems facing their parents. Nick had decided when it was completely settled would be time enough. His attorney was working to get the best deal possible but it still would take away the livelihood he had counted on for the rest of his life.

Josie accepted a position as floor nurse in the post-cardiac ward at St. Rose Hospital and at last Nick seemed to realize that she had worked hard to achieve her goals and deserved to be congratulated.

Danny who was in medical school had also obtained a summer job as aid in the emergency room of the same hospital.

David who was in graduate school studying special education had planned to work for his Dad and was puzzled that he had not heard from him. Jerard whose nickname was J.J. was equally puzzled that he was not offered his old job at the service station.

At last the final papers were signed and the date set to vacate the buildings. Nick sent out memos to each department notifying them of the termination that would be in two weeks. He invited each employee to a luncheon to be held in the restaurant on Saturday. He arranged with the accountant to add another two weeks pay to their final check.

The day of the luncheon, Nick rose to speak to the employees explaining the unavoidable circumstances. "To all of you who have been my friends over the years I say thank you from the bottom of my heart. I wish you the best and will include a letter of recommendation in your final paycheck. This is as devastating to me as it is to you and I can only say God Bless us all."

Nick stayed until the last person had shaken his hand and then he turned and took a last look at his beautiful restaurant and walked slowly into the parking lot.

On a morning in July just two days later a headline in the Denver Post announced that a new multimillion dollar City and County complex was to be built across from the Capitol linking all the government buildings. Details to follow in the business section. There, an artist's drawing of the new complex dominated the page, complete with landscaping and walkways linking the buildings. When the boys came downstairs for breakfast Nick showed them the article.

"For Christ's sake Dad, why didn't you tell us?" Danny was the first to comment.

"Yeah, maybe we could have helped." David chimed in.

Nick took a deep breath, "There was nothing anyone could do, but thanks for the thought." His eyes filled with tears that he was sure embarrassed them even more than it did him. Each of them came to hug him.

A horn sounded in the driveway and Mary Beth came dashing through the kitchen grabbing an apple on her way. She stopped and looked at them, "What's up guys? You look like you lost your last friend."

The horn sounded again and they all laughed and waved her on her way.

Nick felt as though a heavy burden had lifted from his shoulders. They were a great family and somehow they would get through this.

Nick stood in the shade of an old poplar tree, a baseball cap pulled low over his eyes and a jacket long since discarded by one of the boys. Across the street he watched as his work and dreams crumbled brick by brick. The large "Dominics" sign was resting safely in his garage. He had sold all the equipment and furnishings from the restaurant but could not bear to see the sign he had been so proud of go to someone else. The inventory from the station had been sold too so with that money added to what was paid by the government Nick was able to pay off the bulk of his debts. So far it seemed they would be able to keep the house since Josie's job at the hospital could keep them afloat until Nick could decide what to do. Nick continued to watch the demise of his little empire until the big shovels began to scoop up the remains and haul them away.

Nick sat alone in the house. It was the first time in his life that he had nothing to do and nowhere to go. He wandered over to the liquor cabinet and poured himself a straight shot of Jack Daniels and felt the warmth in his belly as it began relax him.

He glanced casually at the clock. My God, it's only ten o'clock and here I am already starting. He thought of his father and how he sat for hours staring into space with the music of the phonograph and the bottle of booze his only companion. Many times he slipped a dollar into Nick's hand and asked him to bring him a bottle from the bar on the corner. He remembered his guilt later when he realized he had contributed to his father's ultimate destruction. Locked up to whither away until his death. Nick shuddered. He felt a sudden urge to see his mother and headed for the garage.

Angela Romano was bent over her sewing machine when Nick tapped at the back door of the little house. She was still as sharp as ever and knew about Nick's business but she would never mention it unless he brought it up. Nick kissed the wrinkled cheek "My son, you come for lunch ? I gotta some pasta fagiolo left-over and good bread, eh?"

"Thanks, Mama." Nick pulled up a chair and watched his mother as she bustled about heating the pasta, slicing bread and pouring coffee from a pot made earlier.

"Everything ok?" the slang word made Nick smile.

"Yeah, ok I guess. I need to find a new business."

His mother nodded. "No good to do nothing. I don't understand why they take your land."

"It's complicated. I've been thinking about papa."

"It was sad I know but you must not think about it. Just be careful so you don't do the same thing. The drinking, it's no good."

"I know Mama, I promise I'll be careful. I won't hurt my family."

They ate lunch and Nick kissed her good-by. He knew what he must do.

The house was quiet when Nick returned. He looked about at the comfortable rooms. Josie had decorated beautifully but never been extravagant. He hoped they could manage to hang on to it. He opened the liquor cabinet and removed a new bottle of Jack Daniels. He gazed at it longingly and then took it to the sink and watched the amber liquid gurgling down the drain. Of course he knew he could get more but it was a symbol that made him proud. He made a pitcher of ice water, poured a tall glass and carried it to the den. From the desk he took a yellow legal pad and sat down and began to write. The words came haltingly at first but then began to fill the pages with his precise penmanship that was a product of his catholic education.

"Hello" Josie called.

"I'm in the den." Nick glanced at the clock. He had no idea he had been writing for three hours.

"What are you doing?" Josies's eyes took in the ice water and written pages. Some crumpled in a pile others neatly stacked.

Nick looked up at her, the gold flecks in his eyes sparkling. "I decided to write a sort of journal about my life." He laughed and the dimple Josie had not seen for a while played in the corner of his mouth.

Josie circled his neck with her arms and kissed his cheek. Nick turned his head so that his lips met hers. He kissed her deeply, his tongue exploring the soft recess of her mouth. He pulled her down on his lap and dropped his head to her breast. She groaned softly and he slid to the floor bringing her with him. The carpet was soft and Josie's nipples tingled and fire raced to her groin. She felt his hardness and fumbled at his belt to unleash it. Their clothes lay in a pile and they reveled in their nakedness. Josie guided him into her and sobbed as she strained against him.

When at last she could speak she whispered "My darling, it has been so long."

"I know and I love you so much." They lay in one another's arms and let the peace and contentment wash over them. "I'm turning over a new leaf and I don't need booze to bolster me."

Josie held him close and kissed his eyes and nose and lips. "It's what I've been praying for." Her voice was soft and intimate. "Right now we'd better get some clothes on before Mary Beth comes flying in" They began to gather up their clothes, laughing like teenagers.

Josie was happier than she had been in a very long time. Her work at the hospital was challenging and although sometimes it was heartbreaking, there were many happy times when patients went home with their families cured of their ailments.

Nick was nearly always home when she returned from work. It seemed strange after all the years of missed dinners and late hours. He continued to write every day with the pitcher of ice water beside him. If the water in his glass occasionally appeared to be tinted light amber, Josie made no mention of it and there was no bottle in evidence. She knew he was doing the best he could and she was grateful.

One afternoon when Josie came into the den Nick had in front of him the medals he had been awarded in the war.

"You haven't looked at those in a long time." Josie picked up one of the boxes and opened it. "The medal you received for saving Paul's life."

Nick nodded, "Do you know that Paul and Sam nor any of the Navajo's ever received any medals at all?"

Josie shook her head.

"The army treated them like nobodies and they contributed as much as any of us probably more. If it hadn't been for them thousands more would have died."

Josie put her arms around Nick from behind "Are you putting that in your memoirs too?"

"Yes, it's always bothered me." Nick gathered up his papers. "I've made *pasta fagioli* for dinner." Josie smiled at this newly changed husband of hers.

At first there were calls from his old cronies. There was always a game in progress in someone's garage or the back of a restaurant but when Nick declined the calls stopped. One Saturday Nick was watching a baseball game on television and Josie sat beside him. "Darling, I was wondering if you would like me to type your manuscript."

"My manuscript?" Nick grinned at her. "It's just a journal. Besides it's pretty personal. Did you think I'd try to publish it?"

"Why not?" She sounded serious. "You might help someone else. It's humorous and yet deeply moving."

"You've read it?"

"Some of it when I was dusting and straightening up. I've done a lot of reading in my life and I'm telling you, it's good."

"Go ahead and type it if you want." He shrugged and went back to the game.

As Josie typed the pages making sure the grammar and spelling were all right and that they were correctly numbered, she became immersed in this account of Nick's childhood, his family and the goings on in a world she had never understood. He made you laugh and then suddenly he changed direction and tears seemed to flow from his pen. It was a chronicle of life, the life of an Italian immigrant's son who wanted above all else to give his sons opportunities that would know no bounds. He was not bitter that his own opportunity had collapsed because he knew it could be done and he was proud that once he had it all.

Money was tight but no one complained. The boys were all working and would soon be back in school with their summer savings supplementing their scholarships. Even Mary Beth was working part-time in a small shop. Nick was now the only member of the family not holding a job. He began to dabble in cooking and with mama's word of mouth recipes he made pasta dishes and soup and even the new American sensation " pizza". The family all enjoyed this new man who was the father they had always admired.

One night in the fall after the boys had returned to their respective schools Josie and Nick were making love before going to sleep when Nick had a sudden and overwhelming pain in his lower abdomen. Josie jumped up to get him something to ease the pain. She ran her hands over his lower body and felt a large lump.

"How long have you had this?" She was surprised she had never noticed it.

"A while, I guess, but it's never really bothered me.

"I think you have a hernia. I'll call the doctor in the morning. You'll probably have to have surgery but it's a simple procedure. Nothing to worry about. Are you feeling all right now?"

"Yes, but it sure spoiled a good time." They snuggled up and were soon asleep.

The surgeon sat behind his desk and shuffled through the papers. "So I've scheduled the surgery for Monday morning at seven. Is that satisfactory?"

They both nodded. "I'd like to ask for the morning off. I'll check with the nursing supervisor today." Josie's stomach dropped at the mere mention of surgery and she thought how different it was when you were talking about family and not just "a patient".

Josie kissed Nick gently and watched as they wheeled him through the large double doors. He was in good spirits and had winked at her as they began pushing the gurney. Josie took her place in the waiting room. A young woman and her husband sat across from her. They held hands and the woman said in a trembling voice. "Our five year old son is in there. He has a tumor on his spine and they think it might be cancer." That dreaded C word, the nurses called it.

"I'm so sorry." Josie said kindly. "I'm a nurse and I see miracles every day and the doctors are excellent so keep up your spirit."

Josie decided to get a cup of coffee in the lounge. She thought she was getting callous but when she saw young people like that with a child in trouble it really hurt.

"Here you are." Mitzi one of the nurses on the floor poked her head in the lounge. "Your sister-in-law is looking for you."

"Anna!" Josie hugged her. "Sit down."

"I thought you'd be in the waiting room."

"I was but I came in here for a cup of coffee."

"Mama wanted to come too, but I talked her out of it. Told her it was just a quickie thing."

"Thanks. It's usually an out patient procedure but since Nick is older the doc figured he'd keep him overnight."

Anna nodded. "Has he been working at all?"

"No, we're managing. He just doesn't seem to be ready."

"Yeah, he never did like working for someone else."

Josie looked at her watch. "I guess we should go back to the waiting room. That's where the doc usually talks to you."

"You're pretty familiar around here aren't you?

"Yeah, I just work one floor down. This Dr. Hartman is a good surgeon."

The young husband and wife were gone. Josie hoped they had good news.

Another hour went by before Dr. Hartman came toward them, still in his surgical greens. "He's in recovery doing ok."

"Thank you."

"I uh need to talk to you, alone, Josie isn't it?"

"This is his sister. You can talk in front of her." A red flag had gone up in her mind and her heart seemed to skip a beat. Something was not right. She knew these doctors and they did not waste time talking unless they had something important to say.

Dr. Hartman led them to the far corner of the room. He looked weary, sweat poured from under his cap and he removed it and wiped his face with it. "I'd give anything not to have to say this but I found cancer cells in Nick's tissue. The hernia itself was not the primary source." He stopped for a minute to see if this was getting across. It was. She's a nurse after all he thought. The sister was puzzled and looked to Josie for confirmation.

"We'll keep him here a few days and do a battery of tests to find out more. This may be a good thing. If he hadn't had the hernia he might have gone on without knowing."

The color had drained from Josie's face and she grabbed the back of a chair for support.

Dr. Hartman put his arm across her shoulder. "We'll do whatever has to be done. We'll get him up tomorrow and I'll leave it up to you whether you want me to tell him or you want to."

Josie dropped her head against the doctor's shoulder for just a moment and then straightened up and took her sister-in-law's hand. "When can we see him?"

"He'll be out of recovery soon and they'll put him back in the room. He did well with the anesthetic but he'll probably sleep most of the day."

"Thanks, we'll wait in his room."

"We'll discuss further treatment tomorrow. I'm really sorry." Dr. Hartman shook his head and left the room. Josie and Anna went to wait for Nicks return.

The following day Nick was informed he would have to stay for some additional tests before he could be discharged. He suspected there was something wrong but was determined to be cheerful for Josie's sake. When she came in to see him he looked at her innocently. "Dammit honey, you should see what they did to my balls. They're black as the ace of spades."

Josie laughed. Leave it to Nick to find some humor in the situation. "So you're going to have a few tests?"

"Yeah, Doc told me more blood work and a liver scan. They drew blood early this morning and should be coming soon to take me to X-ray."

"Okay." Josie looked up as two young men came in with a gurney. "I'll see you later." She kissed him lightly.

Josie told the nurse she would be in the lounge on the floor where she worked so to call her extension when Nick came back.

The phone sat in front of her but Josie was not sure whom she wanted to know the latest development. She would wait to call Anna until she had the results of the scan. The boys didn't need to know anything yet either. She leaned back in the chair alone with her thoughts and fears.

The shrill ring of the phone startled Josie and she opened her eyes and groped for the phone My God I must have fallen asleep." Romano here."

"Josie, you're husband is back from X-ray and Dr. Hartman wants to talk to both of you."

"Thanks I'll be right there."

Nick was sitting in a chair eating a light breakfast. He looked up as Josie entered. "Hi honey. I'm discharged so as soon as the doctor comes and I've finished eating, we can roll."

Dr. Hartman came in looking grim and carrying a piece of paper. He nodded, "I'll get right to it. Your scan showed the liver is highly compromised with cancer cells. We did a needle biopsy that will show us for sure." He paused and watched their faces as Josie went to Nick's side and took his hand. "I have made an appointment with Dr. Chan, the oncologist, to evaluate you for chemotherapy." He handed Josie the paper. "As you know, it's been quite successful, but the liver, well it's a tough one. I'm very sorry."

"Thanks." Nick released Josie's hand and reached up to shake Dr. Hartman's. as he turned and left the room. Nick and Josie stared at each other then Nick rose and took her in his arms. She clung to him briefly.

"Let's get the hell out of this place." Nick's voice was strong and clear.

Chapter XVII
Six Months Later

Nick and Josie had settled into a comfortable routine. They did not dwell on either the consequences or the trauma of what they knew was inevitable. Instead they spent their time becoming more aware of each other. Josie had coordinated her day off with Nick's "chemo" day and they cooked together, read together, watched TV together, went for walks and most important of all they talked. Josie told him of her fears when she found she was pregnant and had no where to go. She told him how kind her aunt and uncle had been and then how scared she was when she knew he was coming home because it had been so long she wasn't sure they would still have feelings for each other, Maybe it had all just been a fantasy. He told her how it was only because of her and the baby that he was able to withstand the horror of the war. He told her how he saw his friends and comrades blown to bits, legs, arms and torsos flying through the air. The men who were shot while landing waist deep in the blood red water and drowned before they could reach the shore. He told her of the filth of the foxholes when they couldn't bathe or change clothes for days on end. The hospital ships with the rows and rows of men crying and moaning in that valley of tears. They spoke of the hopes and dreams they had for their children that they would never have to endure the poverty and horror of war.

And then one day when they had said all there was to say, they settled into a comfortable loving touching silence broken only by the comments of daily life.

The chemotherapy treatments were over but the cancer cells had continued to spread. Dr. Chan had tried everything available and now even he became discouraged. Nick looked thin and tired but never ceased to find humor whenever possible.

The Christmas holidays were nearly here and Josie decided to go all out with elaborate decorations and not one but two trees. The one in the living room was white and gold and appeared to have been confiscated from some designers shop window. Nick laughed when he saw it rise above the windows in sparkling splendor. "Looks too fancy and artificial for our comfortable décor."

Josie stood back and cocked her head, "I think you're right but what's done is done and I'm not taking it down."

The tree in the den was green and smelled of pine and nestled between the fireplace and wood box as though it belonged. The decorations were all the ornaments from years gone by including the ones made by each of the children as they progressed in school.

Josie issued an invitation to each member of the family. Mama, Gina, Anna and Tony and their twin daughters Lily and Lisa and even the elderly aunt and uncle whom they seldom saw. She encouraged Danny to bring his girlfriend who was a fellow-student and David and J.J to bring a friend too. Mary Beth asked if she could bring her best friend whose parents were divorced and whose mother was dating a man who would take her to a fancy restaurant. It was not a conscious thing that this might very well be Nick's last Christmas but it hung in the air much like the subtle odor of pine.

Nick did not feel strong enough to attend Mass and on Christmas Eve. Father Mike himself came to bring Nick the sacred communion wafer and a bottle of dark red wine. Josie left them alone to visit while she prepared a light supper.

When Father Mike had left Nick took Josie in his arms. "Thank you. I needed that." And he kissed her long and lingeringly as though he could not bear to let her go.

Christmas morning was clear and sunny as it often was just before the bitter cold of January. Josie was busy in the kitchen when Danny entered

"Mom I am almost a doctor you know" he grinned shyly "and I'm really worried about Dad. He is having a hard time getting up and I'm thinking he should be in the hospital."

Josie reached up and touched his cheek. "Not today. If he's worse tomorrow I'll call Dr. Chan but let him enjoy today. You and I will help him down the stairs." Her tone was final and Danny nodded agreement.

Nick sat in his usual chair and laughed and joked with all the guests. If he seemed thinner and paler no one mentioned it and when they had all left Josie and Danny helped him up stairs. "Thanks son. You'll make a fine doctor." He gave him a hug and Danny turned quickly to hide the tears in his eyes.

The next morning Josie was scheduled to work. Danny was on Christmas break and Josie knew he would be at Sharon's apartment. She dialed the number. "May I speak to Danny, please?"

"Mom?"

"Danny I need your help. The doctor wants me to bring your Dad in. He wants to start some IV Heparin but Dad begged me not to call an ambulance and I don't think I can get him in the car by myself."

"I'll be right there."

Danny pulled back the covers and was horrified to see his fathers feet were nearly black and knew it was creeping up his legs. Josie and Danny exchanged a look over Nick's head.

Josies eyes reflected a deep sadness while Danny's eyes spelled fear. Nick tried to rise but Danny picked him up in his arms and carried him to the car. Josie grabbed the quilt from the bed and together they settled Nick in the rear seat tucking the quilt around his legs. Josie climbed in beside him and laid her head against his shoulder. As Danny roared out of the garage Nick smiled at Josie and brushed his lips across her forehead.

Nick was settled in a room and Josie was on duty in her unit. Dr. Hartman came in and took her aside. "Dr. Chan called me and I've just been to see Nick. I'm sorry to have to tell you but I think this is very close to the end."

Josie felt as though he had punched her in the stomach. Her eyes pleaded, "The heparin's not working? "

"There's not anything more we can do. He says he's not in pain but his system is slowly shutting down." Dr. Hartman put his arm around her. "Why don't I call your supervisor and get someone to sub for you and you can spend some time with him?"

Josie nodded, "Thanks."

Dr. Hartman patted her arm "I'll take care of it."

Josie entered the room to find Nick sitting up smiling. A tray with jello and tea lay abandoned on his table and he motioned for her to sit beside him and they kissed gently. His skin was pale and waxy and stretched across the fine lines of his handsome face. The cleft in his chin looked deeper and the dimple still played in the corner of his mouth. Her love for him welled up inside her and denied the inevitable.

Later in the day Josie called the boys who came at once to spend some time with their father. Mary Beth came in briefly but left in tears. Josie found her in the lounge sobbing uncontrollably. Josie held her youngest child close and tried to comfort her.

Anna and Tony brought Mama and Gina to visit and the boys left to make room. Josie took this opportunity to run home and change into beige wool slacks and a soft creamy sweater. She threw a few things in a plastic bag in case she ended up staying the night. She was glad they had given Nick a private room although she knew the significance of the gesture.

When Josie returned Nick was sleeping and the visitors were gone. Josie thought how small and thin he looked lying against the white sheets. He is still much too young for this.

The nurse came in to replace the IV and Nick opened his eyes. He saw Josie at once and winked at her as the nurse worked.

"Will you be staying the night?" the nurse asked turning to Josie.

"Yes I will."

"I'll bring a blanket and pillow. Those lounge chairs aren't the most comfortable things but they work."

"Thanks Angie, I'll be fine."

When the nurse finished her duties she brought back the bedding and turned off the light. "Have a good night and if you need anything just put on the light."

"Thanks again."

Josie spread out the blanket but Nick motioned for her and pushing aside the sheet held out his arm. Josie slid in beside him snuggling against him. Nick kissed her nose. "I love you baby." His voice was low and husky with emotion. "It's been a great run. I'm ready."

She looked into his beautiful eyes that always spoke volumes. "I love you too." She reached up and traced his cheek to his lips then raised her head to meet his.

They were soon asleep wrapped in each other's arms.

Josie opened her eyes to the sound of the early morning tasks. The nurse came in armed with the thermometer, a stethoscope around her neck and a new IV. Josie felt the weight of Nick's arm as she started to rise. She knew at once that he had left her sometime during the night. It had not been long because his body was still warm but she and the nurse looked at each other and knew. Josie laid his arm across his chest and the nurse checked his carotid for a pulse. "I'm so sorry."

Josie's face crumpled and tears rolled down her cheeks. She bent and kissed him and tucked the sheet around him. She nodded to the nurse. "I have to make some calls."

Josie went through the motions of arranging a traditional Italian funeral. The Rosary with an open casket and Mama pulling a chair up close to say the prayers she had said for him all the years of his growing. In sickness and war and the good times too.

Others filed by with comments "he looks so natural", "he looks good, like he's asleep," "he's too young to go." Josie sat in the back of the church until everyone had left. She looked at her Nick. She touched his cheek with her finger and let it rest in the cleft of his chin. She let her fingers brush his hair. She gripped his shoulder feeling the soft wool of his suit and thought how many times she had held it while dancing, while leaning over to whisper to him but now it was an empty shell and the man was gone but he would live in her heart forever.

The next morning the church was overflowing with many of the people who had known Nick. The flag-draped casket was brought in followed by Monsignor Fernellie and Father Mike and the rest of the entourage. Four altar boys assisted and the choir's voices resonated through out the church. Friends from his childhood in the coal mining town, customers from the restaurant, people who had patronized his service station for years, teachers and coaches he had come to know from his sons activities, senators, judges and councilmen from the courts across the street filled the pews. Paul had come from Arizona accompanied by Sam Running Horse's son, the doctor, grown up and educated in the white mans way.

It was bitter cold in the cemetery as the group gathered for the last good-bye. The priest's voice shook with cold and emotion and a driving snow fell on the faces and down the necks of those who bowed their heads. The guns roared their salute and the mournful sound of the bugle echoed among the windswept grave stones.

A young Marine in full dress uniform stood in front of Josie and placed the triangle folded American flag in her arms. She clutched it to her breast and flanked by her sons, daughter and family, she turned away, leaving behind the life and the man she had loved for three decades.

Chapter XVIII
One Year Later

Clouds pregnant with moisture rolled and bumped across the gray sky. Dawn pushed its way through in streaks that filtered toward the ground.

The nurses were pouring from the big double doors of the hospital after a long night on duty.

"Sure looks like a storm today." Angie said pulling her jacket around her uniform clad figure.

"Typical December morning." Josie answered. "I have two days off so I'll see you."

"Lucky you. See 'ya later."

Josie headed for her car. Already driving darts of snow were beginning to fall, hitting her face and covering the tops of the cars. Just like the day of Nick's funeral. Josie felt a curtain of sadness closing around her. Stop it, she thought, it's been a whole year. The door handle was freezing and Josie cursed the fact that her gloves were inside the car. She jerked open the door and slid inside. Her gloves were lying on the seat. You're such an idiot. She started the car and waited for the heater to blow warm instead of cold. She sat staring at the windshield as it began to gather snow. It's the seventh of December. She remembered the day the President said it would live in infamy. She hated that day even then. Thirty years later Nick would be buried on that same awful date. The heat was beginning to fill the car and Josie knew she should move but instead she laid her head back and tears ran unheeded down her face. After a minute or so she brushed the tears away with the back of her gloved hand and slowly backed the car out of it's spot, turning on the windshield wipers as she pulled into the street that would take her home.

As she pulled into the driveway, Josie felt a sense of comfort when she saw J.J.'s jeep in the driveway. Lights shone from nearly every window including Mary Beth's bedroom and Josie smiled, knowing her children were home.

"Hi guys. Did you make me some coffee?"

"Hi Mom we sure did." Mary Beth was stuffing her back pack.

"The weather's lousy out there. I had the windshield wipers on the whole way. Be careful driving."

"Peter's picking me up, Mom so don't worry ok?

"Good. Where's J.J.?"

"In Dad's office."

"There's Peter. See you this afternoon, Mom. Get some sleep. Love ya'."

"Bye honey."

Josie took her coffee into the office. J.J. was bent over a stack of papers.

"Hi what's up?"

"Oh Mom, my professor loved Dad's Memoirs so if it's ok with you we're going to send out some query letters to some publishers. Is it ok?"

"Sure, dear, I guess. Do you really think someone might publish them?"

"You never know. My professor is a published author and he says they are funny and sad and very interesting."

"I'm sure your Dad would be very pleased."

"I gotta go Mom. See ya' later." J.J. crammed the papers in his brief case.

"It's snowing out so be careful."

"If it's too bad I'll stay at the dorm. I'll call and let you know."

"Ok dear." Suddenly the house was quiet and empty. Josie went back to the kitchen, set her cup in the sink, locked the door and went upstairs. She brushed her teeth and washed her face and taking a flannel nightgown from the drawer she crawled into bed.

Nick slid into bed beside her and began to kiss her tenderly. First her neck then her eyelids and nose. He cupped her breasts in his hands and suckled each one. She could feel the tingling all the way to her groin. Fluttery kisses on her lips turned passionate and Josie felt his naked body lean and hard and pressed him to her guiding him inside. "I've missed you so much." Tears wet her cheeks and she pressed him tighter. Suddenly, wide awake Josie sat up in bed. Foolishly she felt for Nick but of course he was not there. More tears rolled down her cheeks. Her fingers felt between her legs where it was moist and slippery. She began to massage it gently when suddenly it exploded. "Oh, my God." She sobbed and left her fingers lay against her throbbing vagina until it was quiet. Weak and spent she lay back against the pillow. I never knew that could happen. Of course I've heard of masturbating but this.....! She hugged the pillow to her. It was embarrassing but who would know. She laughed aloud, "I must have really needed it."

The telephone rang sharply and Josie reached for it. "Hello." Her voice was barely audible.

"Josephine?"

Only one person called her that. "Paul?"

"I'm sorry I can hardly hear you. Are you all right?"

"Yes, I'm just waking up. I worked all night."

"I'm sorry if I woke you."

"No, honestly I was awake. It's time I got up." She glanced at the clock. It was after three. She had slept for eight hours. She hadn't done that for ages.

"I'm in Denver for a conference and I wondered if we could have dinner."

Josie pulled back the drape. It had snowed all night but now the sun shone brightly.

"Paul would you mind taking a taxi out here?"

"Of course not but I didn't want you to have to cook."

"I promise I won't fuss. I hate driving when the streets are either slushy or slippery."

"Ok then, it's a deal. I should be through by six. Is that too early?"

"Not at all. See you then. Good-bye."

Josie hopped out of bed. Six o'clock, she had better get on the ball. She made coffee to wake herself up and looked outside. They had plowed the street in front of the house but the walkway to the front door was still covered. She'd have to shovel. The answering machine was blinking and when she checked neither of her offspring would be home that night. After all they were both of age and had rooms at the university but secretly she was glad. She and Paul could talk easily of old times and new ventures.

The doorbell chimed at half past six. Josie opened it quickly. Paul wore no hat and his black hair was brushed back from his forehead. He wore a light gray trench coat over a navy suit. He smiled and reached for both her hands.

"I'm sorry I'm late. I didn't think it would take so long to get here. The streets are not the best."

"I was afraid of that." Josie took his hands in hers. "You're freezing. Come in and let me take your coat."

Josie led him into the living room where a fire cast a soft glow on the comfortable furniture and gleaming tables. A plate of hors d'oeuvres and two wineglasses graced the coffee table. She took a bottle of Chardonnay from a silver bucket. "Is this all right?"

"Fine." Paul watched her pour the pale golden liquid. Her hair was gold too he thought, and her eyes looked even bluer than he remembered. She wore a hostess gown of midnight blue velour and a gold bracelet circled her arm. An emerald and gold ring sparkled on her right hand but on her left the wedding ring was gone.

They talked easily of many things and carried their wineglasses to the table. Josie served a hearty casserole of chicken and wild rice, green beans and a salad.

They went back to the living room for coffee and brandy and the Italian pizzelles that she knew Paul had grown to love in his years with Nick.

"Josephine, I have a proposition to make to you."

Josie's eyebrows rose.

"No, nothing indecent I assure you." They were both smiling now. "I wondered if you could come to Arizona and give us some input on the new clinic. The doctor is really very good but the nurses seem so disorganized. We try to use as many natives as possible but many are only locally educated and I don't know what's wrong but there seems to be something missing. I am on the board but I still I have my own job as a teacher and I don't know what to do."

Josie looked at Paul's earnest face and wanted to make the sadness in his dark eyes go away. She wondered what his life was like, living alone in his cinderblock house, being torn between his heritage and the White Man's world. Josie leaned forward.

"I don't know if I could help but I would like to try. I couldn't go until after Christmas but I can ask for a months leave of absence and come in January if they approve it."

"Thank you so much for even considering it. I'll square it with administration when you know for sure. By the way, do you have to work tomorrow?"

"No, I'm off for three days. I go back on days after that."

"Well I guess I'd better call a cab and get going."

"Paul, I have a perfectly good guest room. In fact you've stayed in it before so why not just stay tonight?"

"I-I don't know if it's uh proper."

"Of course it is. You're one of Nick's oldest friends."

"But I have nothing with me."

"No buts. Come upstairs and I'll get you settled. There are toiletries under the vanity. Toothbrush too. I always keep a new one for guests. Please make yourself at home."

"Thank you, Josephine. Goodnight."

"Goodnight Paul."

Josie went back downstairs to check the dishwasher and turn out the lights. The fire was a mere ember but as a precaution she sprayed it with water they kept by the wood box. It sizzled and went out leaving the room in darkness.

There was no light from under Paul's door. Josie went to her own room. She tossed aside the flannel nightgown and chose a violet satin with spaghetti straps. *What am I doing?* Still it made her feel sexy and glamorous and it had been a long time since she had felt that way.

Josie dozed and woke again to find she had only been asleep for two hours. *I slept too long yesterday and now I'm going to have trouble falling asleep.* She would go down stairs and get a glass of milk.

As she passed Paul's door, she felt a blast of cold air. His door was open and the nightlight cast shadows across the room. Josie peeked inside. Paul was sitting in front of the window that was wide open.

"Are you all right?"

Paul jumped up clad only in his briefs. "I'm sorry. I was so warm I was sweating so I decided to get some fresh air. Did I wake you?"

"No, I was heading downstairs for a glass of milk. Can I get you anything?"

Josie shivered in the cold air and Paul pulled a blanket from the bed and put it around her shoulders. She turned toward him and suddenly she was in his arms. "Oh, Jo, I want you so."

His breath caught in his throat and he kissed her. When she responded he held her closer. He laid her carefully on the bed and ran his hands over her body. Her nipples were hard against his lips and he kissed the full length of her body. She grasped his hair and pulled his head back to her breast. She moaned softly as he gently inserted himself inside her. He cried out as she began to push against him and then they came together in a burst of ecstasy. They lay still, not wanting to disturb the closeness between them until they fell asleep. Two lonely people starved for love and intimacy.

The next morning Josie awakened as Paul came out of the bathroom. He was fresh and clean and fully dressed. He sat beside her. "What can I say? Not that I'm sorry because it was the most beautiful thing that has ever happened to me but I am sorry if I took advantage of you."

"Paul it was not just you. I wanted it too. Please don't let this spoil our friendship. I'll still ask for that leave of absence and come to Arizona."

"Thank you."

"Call me." Josie lifted her head and kissed him gently. "Now get going but I'll talk to you soon."

Paul went out the door without looking back.

Christmas was difficult. Memories of other years clouded the joy of the season and only Danny and Christy's toddler kept them laughing as he tore open his gifts. Josie was glad when it was over.

New Years Day was no better except that Josie worked and as usual the hospital was flooded with those who had eaten and drunk too much and ended up with gastritis and injuries from fender benders caused by careless drivers.

At last the dreaded holidays were over and Josie went to see the supervisor with her proposal of a months leave of absence.

Sister Mary Margaret was sympathetic and agreed to the time off but when Josie told her about the plan to reorganize the Indian Clinic, she shook her head.

"That is no way to rest and recuperate from your husbands death." Her voice was kind but stern.

"I just thought I needed a change and if I can do some good at the same time I should be able to get my mind off myself."

"I'm afraid you will find it very difficult. The Indians do not think as we do and it will not be easy to convince them of your ways."

Josie could not help but feel deflated. "I'd still like to try."

"Then good luck, my dear, and come back to us." Sister rose from her desk and shook Josie's hand.

Josie called Paul with the news and he was elated. "I've made arrangements for you to stay at a Bed and Breakfast run by a very nice woman whose daughter is in our program. You'll have a private room and bath and two meals."

"Thanks Paul. Do you think I should drive so I will have a car?"

"I don't think you'll need one as the house is in walking distance of the clinic and if you need one for shopping or what ever you can borrow mine, ok?"

"Sounds great. Are you sure I can do this Paul?"

"I'm positive. Call me as soon as you know the time of your flight and Josephine, I can't wait to see you "

Chapter XIX
Arizona

Paul and Josie bounced along the highway from Flagstaff to Window Rock. The day was crisp and clear and the sun shone on the cliffs and pine trees and warmed the inside of the jeep. Paul had greeted her by taking her into his arms and kissing her upturned face. She leaned against him now feeling comfortable and smiled. "I had no idea it was so beautiful here. I thought Arizona was a desert."

"And so it is but you are in the mountains here." He pulled off the road and they sat looking at the red rocks protruding from the deep green forest. The only sound was the honking of some geese flying over head. "I'm so glad you came." Paul pulled her close and brushed his lips against her hair.

"Oh, Paul, it's so peaceful here." Josie pulled his head down and kissed him. "Thank you for bringing me here. I really needed a change." Paul started the jeep and they continued on their way but Paul knew this was what he had been waiting and wanting for a long time.

The nursing assistants from the *Window Rock Indian Clinic* were not happy about coming to a class after working hours to be taught by a white woman. They sat with sullen faces staring straight ahead.

Josie had already assessed many of the problems and after talking to Maggie her landlady's daughter, she was sure she could help if they would just give her a chance. Nearly all the girls were overweight and Josie had decided that was one reason they appeared slow and even slovenly. Her first goal was to get them interested in exercise and nutrition. Diabetes was prevalent on the reservation and needed to be addressed. It was going to be a monumental under taking, that was for sure.

The days flew by and Josie's program caught on. They were actually having fun and their work ethic was improving at a rate that made Miss Simpson, the supervisor, really take notice. She caught Josie in the cafeteria one day after noting the change of menu

"I don't know what you're doing but whatever it is keep doing it. Nearly every worker is improving and by the way, thanks for getting the cook to put some new items on the menu."

Josie grinned. "I'm glad it's helped. I'll be leaving soon so I hope they keep it up."

Paul and Josie had become very good friends and lovers too even though that had not been in the proposition. In fact Josie was not sure it was proper but after all she was a widow and he was a single man. She had been so busy at the clinic that she did not stop to analyze how deeply she was becoming involved. It was February and in Arizona that meant spring. The cacti on the desolate plains burst into blooms of pink and orange. Blue and yellow bushes spread their limbs across the paths that led to the town's center. The whole area had dressed for spring and girls in colorful skirts flirted and teased the young men who hung out in the streets dressed in the white mans costume of jeans and tee-shirts. Many were drinking beer from aluminum cans that were tossed aside as they became empty.

Paul watched silently then turned to Josie. "We've got to find a way to educate our young men"

"Most of them don't even want to finish high school."

"I know but if we could send them on to a college for men of their own race and teach them trades as well as book learning that might motivate them. An old chief many years ago said *My child, education is a ladder, climb it* and he was so right.

Josie looked at Paul in admiration. First the clinic and now a college just for Indians. He was a very dedicated man. She squeezed his hand.

He squeezed back. "I've been ask to serve on a committee to try and establish a Community College right here in Window Rock."

"Paul that's wonderful."

They had come to the restaurant and as they sat down Josie wondered if Paul remembered that her month was nearly up and she would be returning to Colorado. He was looking at her intently and spoke softly.

"I'm going to miss you so much." Paul covered her hand with his. "Are you sure you can't stay longer?"

Josie laughed aloud. "I'm afraid not. You remember me telling you that Mary Beth is getting married and I have a wedding to plan. Then J.J. called and a publisher is interested in Nick's Memoirs. They want us to sign a contract so I contacted Mr. Ingle, Nick's attorney, and we have a meeting scheduled for next week."

"You do have a lot on your plate." Paul looked forlorn. Josie touched his cheek.

"We'll keep in close touch and of course you'll come to the wedding."

Paul nodded and put his hand on hers and brought it to his lips.

Chapter XX
Colorado

Josie had to admit that it was good to be home in her own place with her own things. Today was the meeting with the publisher and J.J. had promised to be here so he could accompany her. She was nearly ready to give up when he came rushing in. His hair was mussed and he seemed unusually nervous. "Sorry I'm late."

"We'll take my car." Josie picked up her keys and J.J. followed.

The negotiations went very well. Mr. Kohl from the publishing firm and Mr. Ingle their attorney worked out any small glitches and Josie listened carefully. One thing the publisher was insistent about was that Josie go on a tour to promote the book. Especially since it was non-fiction and the author deceased he felt that a member of the family must go. Josie suggested J.J. since he had done the work so far but he looked terrified.

"I couldn't possibly go." He insisted. "Mom is so much more poised and certainly knew Dad and his life much better."

Josie agreed with one exception. It was not to interfere with Mary Beth's wedding. Mr. Kohl concurred and wrote the date into the contract.

"It will be some time before the book is ready anyway. There is much to do. We edit, apply for the copyright, the ISBN number and all the other little details. Our publicity department will arrange the tour and one of the young ladies in the department will accompany you."

"Then it's settled." Josie and Mr. Kohl shook hands.

As they left the room Mr. Ingle complimented Josie. "You did well in there and stand to make a good deal of money."

"If the book sells." Josie said smiling.

"Yes, well that's business. By the way you look stunning today and I think you really impressed the New Yorker."

Josie smiled again. "Thank you for everything." They shook hands.

"Call me if you have any questions. Nice to meet you, son." He shook J.J.'s hand and hurried down the steps.

Spring had come quickly after the cool March winds and now the pink blossoms on the flowering plum trees spread their fragrance across the yard and into Josie's open window. She breathed deeply. It was a perfect time for love and romance.

The wedding was beautiful and Mary Beth a vision in her silk dress trimmed in tiny pearls. Peter was dashing in his tux and the bridesmaids pale green gowns were perfect for spring. Only her Daddy's absence marred Mary Beth's complete happiness but she felt his presence and knew he must surely be watching. Danny proudly walked his sister down the aisle and handed her off to her waiting groom.

Paul had come to the wedding but due to all the activities Josie had seen very little of him. At last at the reception they danced and it felt wonderful to be in his arms once more.

"I've missed you." Paul whispered against her hair. His lips brushed her forehead.

"I've missed you too." She pressed close to him. "Maybe we can meet someplace while I'm on the tour."

"You sound like a pro." He smiled down at her. "Just say the word and I'll come anywhere."

"I just might do that." They danced in silence holding each other close.

As the music ended Paul released her reluctantly.

"I can't believe that I'm really going on a tour to promote Nick's book. Josie shook her head in wonderment. "You're in it, you know. He loved you like a brother."

"I want to read it but it will bring back so many memories."

"I know, it did for me too." Josie rose from the chair. "I must get back to the guests."

"Josephine please keep in touch." Paul's voice was husky with emotion.

"I promise. Good by for now."

It was decided that the newlyweds would stay in the house at least until Josie returned from the book tour. J.J. had taken an apartment in Boulder where he attended some post grad classes and worked for the newspaper. Josie felt free and exhilarated. She could not remember ever having been on a trip alone. Of course she would hardly be alone. Mr. Kohl had assigned a publicist and photographer to accompany her. She was flying to Los Angeles where she would meet them and begin the tour.

The book tour proved to be very exciting. Josie had read the finished book from cover to cover and discovered things that even she had not known about Nick's life and the life of his mother and father. It was very humorous in places and very poignant in others. It brought tears to her eyes and she knew what the publisher meant when he said it would appeal to all the people who had been brought up in that era. The section about the war was the same way. Some of it was very funny but the battle scenes were so real Josie could almost feel the bullets whizzing by and smell the stench of dead bodies. He had captured it all.

The producers of the shows they appeared on were very pleased with Josie. She was attractive, photogenic and a good conversationalist. Tiffany, Josie' s companion on the tour was a good organizer and extremely savvy when it came to handling the details of the TV shows and book signings. Josie liked Tiffany and they were not unlike a mother and daughter as they began to share confidences. Tiffany's dream was to become a writer preferably of screen plays but in the meantime just being in the business was exciting. She had left her parents and boy friend behind and gone to Hollywood to pursue her dream.

Josie told Tiffany about her family and teased that it was too bad J.J. had not come on the tour since the two of them had so much in common.

" J.J. has never really had a steady girl. He is a reporter but like you he would like to write plays. If it hadn't been for him, his Dad's book would have still be lying in the drawer."

Just then the phone rang. "It's for you Mrs.R." Tiffany said as she handed her the phone.

"Mom, how are things going?" J.J.'s voice was animated. "I saw you on that entertainment news show. You were great".

"Thanks, dear. What's up?"

"Mom I hate to ask this but I was wondering if you could float me a loan. I got this new apartment and I need some stuff and I still owe for my books."

"Of course, you know I told you that I had Mr. Ingle put you in the contract as my agent so you'll probably be getting some checks but until then how much do you need?"

"About five thousand if it's ok."

Josie felt a tinge of discomfort. That was a lot of money. "Sure, ok I'll have the bank transfer it to your checking account first thing in the morning."

"Thanks, Mom. I love you."

"Love you too. Bye."

Josie sat on the edge of the bed. She felt suddenly tired. All this traveling was getting to her.

"Everything ok?" Tiffany had come in with the next day's itinerary.

"I guess. J.J. needs some money. I hope everything is all right."

The tour was finally winding down. They were in New York and tomorrow would be the biggest day yet. Josie would be appearing on the "Today" show and then after a book signing they would be nearly finished. Tiffany had gone shopping with her and she had splurged on an emerald green silk suit and an expensive ivory blouse. She had her hair and nails done in the hotel's salon and heaved a big sigh of relief at the thought that she would soon be going home.

Josie had to admit that New York was an exciting place. The buildings were so tall you could hardly see the sky and yet right across from the hotel was this luscious green park. The women she saw on the streets and coming in and out of the stores all looked like models. She couldn't help but contrast it to the barren desert of Arizona and the mountains of Colorado. Josie wished that she could see Ellis Island and thought maybe they could manage to squeeze some time for it after the book signing.

"You're going to knock 'em dead tomorrow." Tiffany grinned as she glanced at the clothes ready and waiting for tomorrows show.

Josie placed a call and waited for Paul to pick up the phone. She had promised to keep in touch but it had been such a whirlwind tour that she scarcely ever had a minute to herself. She wondered if it would be possible for them to meet somewhere. Maybe he would have an idea. Finally his voice came on the line, cool and professional. *You have reached Dr. Paul Begay. Please leave your name and number after the tone.*

She knew that Paul had earned his PHD some time ago but she had never heard him called Doctor in their relationship. She smiled as she thought of how far he had come and wondered if at last it didn't matter that he was Indian. She was disappointed that he didn't answer but really had no message so she hung up.

Josie and Tiffany came back to the hotel after an especially long and tiring day. They had arisen very early for the appearance on the "TODAY" show. It had been a good interview and Josie had indeed looked stunning in her new suit. From there they had a book signing at a huge Manhattan bookstore. The crowds were astonishing and the line went halfway around the block. Tiffany said that for an unknown author it was phenomenal. Josie was relieved that the tour was nearly over. She was bone tired, and throwing her jacket on the chair, she lay across the bed.

"Josie." Tiffany shook her shoulder. "I'm sorry to wake you but your son is on the line and says it's very important."

Josie sat up trying to get her bearings. She took the phone and cleared her throat. "Hello."

"Mom!" She came quickly awake.

"Danny? What is it?" She knew his voice that was always so calm now sounded so desperate. "Has something happened to the children?"

"No Mom, it's J.J. He's had a seizure. He's in the hospital. He's unconscious."

"I don't understand. A seizure? My God what happened?"

"Mom can you get a plane out tonight? I'm trying to handle it but we need you."

"Let me see what I can do. I'll be there as soon as possible. Give me the hospital phone number and I'll call you as soon as I can make arrangements."

Tiffany took over and found a flight to Denver at eight. She called a cab and packed a small carry-on. Josie was shaking so she could scarcely speak. "I'm usually very good in emergencies but this is just so unexpected."

"It's all right. I'll take care of things and call Mr. Kohl. There was only one more signing and then we were going to leave anyway. Our tour is finished."

Josie hugged her companion who had also become her friend. "Thank you Tiffany. I'll be in touch."

When the plane touched down in Denver all the fear and apprehension came crowding back. She hurried down the ramp and into the terminal. She heard Mary Beth shouting her name and started toward her. Newspaper reporters swarmed around her. "What brings you here? Did you cut your tour short? Is there some sort of emergency?" She had forgotten how reporters knew everything. She had become a recognizable face from her TV appearances.

"No comment!" She pushed through them to Mary Beth and Peter. Shielding her with their bodies they hurried to the police car waiting outside. "They're friends of mine." Peter said, "they'll get us to the hospital pronto." Josie had forgotten he was a deputy prosecutor.

The hospital was quiet and looked deserted. The intensive care unit was down a long narrow hall on the third floor. On a bench outside the door Danny sat with his head in his hands. Hearing their steps he rose to greet his mother. He held her tightly in his arms.

"Are you going to tell me what's going on?" Josie's voice was scolding as though he were a child.

"I'm sorry Mom. I didn't want to tell you on the phone. It was a drug overdose."

153

Josie stared at him. "What do you mean? He didn't take drugs."

Danny looked miserable. "He's been taking drugs for a long time. He started in high school. I'm sorry, I tried many times to stop him, but he always said he had it under control"

Josie looked at her son in disbelief. He couldn't have. She would have known.

"I want to see him."

Danny pressed the direct line to ICU "J.J.'s mother has arrived. She would like to see him."

The door swung open. The room was circular with smaller rooms forming a glass enclosed circle around a nurse's station. The nurses could see into every room. The nurse led her to the third room on the right. Was that really J.J.? Josie would never have recognized him if she had not been led to him. He was as white and still as the sheets that covered him. Patches of his hair had been shaved away so they could attach the wires that measured his brain waves. Josie bent over him until her face was only inches from his.

"Hi darling, it's Mommy." As a nurse, Josie knew that many times people who were in a coma could hear you even if they could not react. She tried again. Louder this time. "Wake up J.J. I've come home."

"Please wake up. Blink your eyes, darling!" Finally she took his hand and squeezed it and sank into the chair beside the bed. She stayed there until at last the nurse led her away.

"Get some rest and come back later." She said kindly.

Danny took her from the nurse. How could he get her to go home and rest? She was going to collapse if she didn't sleep and eat. She looked up at him and her voice was like steel.

"Why didn't I know? I *always* worried about alcohol. Your grandfather was an alcoholic and I knew you might all have the tendency so I kept my eyes open watching for signs of drinking but I never saw the drugs. It's the addictive nature. Some people are born with it but I thought you were all safe. I should have seen it."

"It isn't your fault."

"Oh, yes it is. Mother's are supposed to notice things like that. What was I doing? Going to school, working? Nothing is more important than your children."

"Mom please."

Josie cut him off. "Take me home now. I'm going to take a shower and go to bed but tomorrow I'm coming back and I'm going to stay with J.J. until he wakes up."

Josie was as good as her word. Weeks went by and every day she went to the hospital. She talked to the doctors and when they gave her no hope she called the neurosurgeon at St. Rose where she worked and asked him to come and give his evaluation. In the meantime she talked to J.J. constantly and rubbed his hands and feet.

Dr. John Rosenberg tapped on the door of J.J.'s room. Josie rose to greet him.

"It was good of you to come, Doctor."

He took both of Josie's hands in his. "I've reviewed the Electrocardiogram, the Brain Scan and all the tests and I'm sorry to tell you that I concur with the diagnosis. Your son's brain is irrevocably damaged. There is no activity, the line is flat."

At Josie's gasp, he pressed her hands tighter. "I wish there was something I could do but as difficult as it is I'm afraid you will have to let him go. He is not alive, Josie. Only the respirator is doing the breathing."

The pain in Josie's eyes was unbearable. The doctor let go of her hands and put his arms around her. "I'm so sorry."

The following morning Danny and the administrator brought papers for Josie to sign. As she finished signing them the nurse came in. "Why don't you go have a cup of coffee while I make J.J. more comfortable."

Josie wanted to scream at her. How do you make someone comfortable who cannot feel? Of course she knew the drill. Take out all the tubes and make the patient *look* more comfortable.

A few minutes later Josie resumed her seat and seeing her son lying there with no hope for the future she put her head on the bed and sobbed.

Danny brought her a glass of water and some tissues and Josie continued to sit quietly. Danny stood near the door. "I've got to get some work done. I'll be back later." He dropped a kiss on her cheek and closed the door.

Josie had no idea how long she had been there but it must have been hours. Deep shadows filled the room and someone had turned on a dim light. She heard Nick's voice. *You did the right thing, dear. Don't worry about J.J. I'll take good care of him.* Josie opened her eyes with a start. She was sure she had heard her son take a deep breath. Then she heard the inevitable release of the bodily fluids and she knew that her beautiful son had truly gone to another place.

The funeral was small and private with only members of the immediate family.

Nick's mother looked confused and intolerably sad. Her son and grandson had gone before her. It was not the way of life's circle. For the first time since she had come into the family Josie saw her mother-in-law give up. She had been through so many hardships in her long life but this had taken its toll. Josie held her close but it was she who comforted Josie.

"He will be with the angels and his family." She said and Josie kissed her wrinkled cheek.

At last it was over and Josie retreated to her room. Staring out the window at the red and gold leaves brushing their delicate fingers against the glass pane Josie wondered how she could cope after losing her husband and her son. How would she ever get her life back on track?

Chapter XXI
Colorado
One Year Later

Josie sat at the desk in the den. She still thought of it as Nick's desk. He had poured out his heart and soul here knowing all the while that death was waiting just around the corner. His book had been on the New York Times Best Seller list for over a year and was still selling in the thousands and bringing in royalties. His mother had died shortly after J.J.'s death. Losing her son and grandson had been too much for her ninety-five year old heart and she had slipped away in her sleep.

Josie was catching up on some correspondence and was staring blankly at the page of paper. So much had happened since Nick's death. Josie still could not reconcile J.J.'s sudden death. She still felt guilt that if she had been more observant he would still be alive. She could have arranged for rehab. Many patients that she knew had kicked the habit and were living productive lives. He could have been one of them. How she had missed seeing any of the signs she couldn't fathom. She sighed deeply. Her supervisor at the hospital had suggested that she seek therapy for her guilt and anger and so she was now in the process of pouring out her heart to the kindly gray haired woman who listened intently but had yet to give her a solution.

Josie had thrown herself into her work that had not seemed to suffer from her own feelings. She had been transferred from the ICU unit to a "post" coronary unit. The assignment was known as a "breeze" by many of the nurses because about all there was to do was pass medications and keep up the spirits of the mostly male patients who felt that their life had been changed forever by a heart attack and its subsequent surgical procedure.

Josie surprised herself by being very understanding and sympathetic to these patients. Sometimes she even got tough with them and told them how lucky they were to be alive.

It was spring again. The months seemed to go on even though Josie sometimes felt she was standing still. David had married in a small intimate wedding to a girl he had gone with since high school. Mary Beth and Peter had stayed on here at the house and their baby girl was a joy. She was a happy baby and Josie enjoyed the sounds of cooing and laughing. It seemed to make the house and life a little more bearable.

"Mom." Mary Beth's voice brought her out of her reverie. "It's the phone for you."

Josie sighed.

"It's Paul, Mom. The poor man calls regularly and you never talk to him. He sounds miserable."

It was true of course. She had barely spoken to him since J.J.'s death. She wasn't sure why. It certainly had nothing to do with him. It was her weird feelings. It was as though she did not deserve the joy she had felt with him.

Slowly she picked up the phone. "Hi."

"Josephine. It's wonderful to hear your voice. How are you?"

"OK, I guess. Sorry I've been so hard to get."

Paul laughed softly. "You're hard to get all right."

Josie had to laugh too. "I didn't mean that the way it sounded."

"I know. Really though I hope you're doing better."

His voice sounded so kind and loving. "Oh Paul, I'm not doing good at all. I'm even seeing a shrink." Suddenly she was sobbing.

There was complete silence as he waited for her to get control. When her sobs had subsided to a sniffle Paul spoke. "Jo darling please may I come and see you?"

At that moment she could think of nothing she wanted more than to have his arms around her. In a small voice she answered. "Yes, come as soon as possible."

As he hung up the phone Paul closed his eyes. He had been patient and tried not to rush her and now at last she wanted him. Not only did she want him she needed him. He had so wanted to comfort her and now she was asking for his help. He found himself trembling with anticipation. He had so many things to tell her, so many surprises. Could his love bring her out of her depression and back to his world? Almost immediately he began planning for the trip to Colorado. Would she be willing to come back with him? The past year Paul had let the old demon of race rear its ugly head. He thought that maybe she was sorry she had become his lover. After all, the Indian in him said, she did not want him in her world because she seemed so happy to go home again. When her son died, she had stopped communicating, Paul had nearly given up. She was back with her own people and probably felt that her time in Arizona with him had been a mistake or at most just an interlude. None of that mattered now his Josephine needed him.

Josie stared at the phone. What had she done? She had decided that her time in Arizona with Paul had been a mistake. She belonged here in Colorado where she had spent her married life and where her children and grandchildren still lived.

Now she was practically begging Paul to come here and start up all the old feelings. They lived in two separate worlds. She had tried to be one of them and it had failed. Maggie had told her once that she could never know how it felt to walk in her shoes. Tradition was the most important aspect of Indian life. Josie went to ceremonial observations for birth, death and marriage and tried to understand why tradition was more important than progress. The Indians that Josie knew were intelligent human beings. Surely they could see that proper nutrition was needed for diabetics and pre natal care for mothers. So why did they still depend on the shama when someone was ill instead of bringing them to the clinic?

Paul was different, or was he? He stayed on at the reservation and she knew that he participated in some of the ceremonies. She had never seen him in any of the "Indian Regalia" but she knew he possessed some costumes and artifacts belonging to his family.

Paul called to say that he was driving to Colorado and would arrive before noon on Saturday.

When the doorbell chimed Josie rose with a start. Her heart was beating rapidly and she opened the door to see Paul standing before her. He was dressed casually in brown slacks and suede leather jacket, the color of a young doe. His dark hair was brushed back from his forehead and his brown eyes met hers. He smiled shyly and held out his hand to her but she threw her arms around him.

"I'm so glad to see you." Josie's voice had a slight tremor and as she looked up at him her eye's filled with tears.

He held her close. He had not expected this reaction and he was overcome with emotion and kissed her eyes and found her lips salty from the tears. Paul pushed the door closed with his foot and half-carried her to the nearest chair. His lips had never left hers and now he held her on his lap. She snuggled her body next to his and they finally parted lips long enough to take a breath. He kissed her neck and the cleavage between her breasts

"The kids are gone for the afternoon." Josie said breathlessly and began to take the jacket from his shoulders. Paul unbuttoned her blouse and buried his face. He kissed each breast and let his tongue brush them. She moaned softly and gripping his hair she pulled him harder against her. She could feel his hardness and struggled to unzip his trousers. They fell on the soft carpeting and touched each other in every nook until he inserted himself into her. When they lay back exhausted Josie looked around her at the clothes strewn in disarray and at their naked bodies gleaming with sweat, she laughed. "I missed you Paul."

Paul had felt such ecstasy flowing through his body he could barely speak.

"That was quite a welcome." He swallowed to keep his own emotions from the surface.

Quickly they began to gather up their clothes and Josie motioned him to follow her up the stairs and into the bathroom. She turned on the water in the shower and they stepped inside closing the glass door behind them.

Fully dressed and composed Josie and Paul sat at the kitchen table sipping freshly brewed coffee.

"I have so much to tell you." Paul said quietly. "I've had so many changes in my life the past few months."

"Really?"

"Yeah, but I would like you to come to Arizona and check it out for yourself. Maggie is receiving her degree in Nursing from the University and she would love it if you came to see her graduate."

"Well, I haven't taken any vacation time since I took the new assignment in the coronary unit."

"Then you will come back with me?"

"If they can get someone to cover for me, I'll ask for a few days vacation."

Paul grinned as wide as she could ever remember. "Come outside and see my first surprise." He pulled her to her feet.

Sitting in the driveway was a beautiful new Buick. It was the color of the desert and the chrome trim gleamed in the sunlight.

"Wow!" Josie smiled up at him. "It's gorgeous! Where's your jeep?"

"Oh, I keep it for roaming around the desert. Let's take a ride and stop someplace for dinner."

"OK, let me leave a note for the kids."

Josie leaned back in the soft leather seat. For the first time in over a year she felt completely relaxed and happy.

Chapter XXII
Arizona

The desert landscape fell away as Paul and Josie made the ascent to Flagstaff and one could scarcely see daylight through the lush branches of the pine trees and high above, the San Francisco Peaks still showed remnants of last winter's snowfall.

The trip had been pleasant and relaxing. They had talked about guilt and how it affected their lives. Paul still lived with the guilt of Sam's death, feeling that if it had not been for his suggestion that Sam join him in enlisting in the Marines, he would still be alive to raise his children and tend his ranch. Then there was Morning Star. If only he had driven her to a hospital she would have had the baby surgically and both of them would have lived. He would never forget the sight of his wife lying in a pool of blood and the tiny babe that was his son not crying, not breathing, just silent and still.

Josie's guilt was fresher but just as devastating. She should have seen the signs of drug abuse and found a way to stop it. Her handsome sensitive brilliant son was taken from this world by the ugly curse of drug addiction.

They pulled into a beautiful Holiday Inn. Josie could not remember ever having seen it before. "Is this new?" She was remembering the dilapidated motel they had stayed in when she first came to Arizona.

"Yes, it's only been here a year or so. Many tourists stop here on the way to the Grand Canyon so I would guess it has paid off."

The young man who came to park the car grinned. "She's a beauty, sir." He was scanning the new car from front to back.

Paul tossed him the keys.

Paul took two small bags from the trunk and they went inside.

The clerk smiled, "Dr. Begay. It is nice to see you. Your reservation did not specify if you wish two beds or a king."

Paul was hesitant and Josie answered. "A king will be fine."

The lobby was stunning. It was done in Indian design and opposite from the gift shop was a scene depicting an Indian Brave mounted on a horse with mountains behind him and a young deer poised by a stream with real water running through it. The statuary was very well done and looked almost real. Indian artifacts and paintings adorned the walls. Josie stood staring at the scene until she noticed the bellboy standing by the elevator with their luggage. Then she turned and joined Paul. "It is so beautiful and realistic."

"Yes, it's rather nice that they are using the American Indian motif after all these years."

The room was as spectacular as the lobby and the bed looked so comfortable that Josie sat on its edge and kicking off her shoes lay back on the huge pillows.

"I could use a little nap before we go down for dinner." Josie said in a soft voice. She patted the bed beside her and Paul came and lay by her side. He pulled her close and kissed her.

"You've made me the happiest guy on the planet." He whispered against her hair. "Just being with you."

The graduation was inspiring and Josie was amazed at how many people Paul seemed to know. Maggie was already in line when she glimpsed them in the crowd and smiled and waved. Her mother Singing Bird was sitting in the front row smiling proudly.

As they watched student after student receive their degrees Josie observed that there were only six students that appeared to be Indian or Hispanic. It seemed a dismal percentage.

As soon as the ceremony was over Maggie and her mother came toward them.

"I'm so glad you came." Maggie was euphoric.

"Congratulations." Paul shook her hand.

"I'm so proud of you." Josie gave her a warm hug.

"I would have never done it without you Ms Romano. Please come to the restaurant and join us for some refreshments, okay? It's the *Casa Bonita.* Do you know it?"

"Sure, we'll be there." Paul took Josie's arm and guided her through the crowd. He stopped briefly to speak to several people and when they were back in the car he squeezed Josie's hand.

"Thank you for being here today."

After checking out of the hotel Paul and Josie stopped by the restaurant. It was in a neighborhood of small run-down shops and motels. The restaurant was noisy, opaque with smoke and smelled of grease. As they entered several young men from the reservation stood languidly drinking beer and girls from the school and hospital greeted them. In the back of the restaurant a table was set up with a bright blue tablecloth. A cake in the center read *Congratulations Maggie.* There were trays of food and a stack of paper plates, plastic utensils and paper napkins. On one end a colorful basket held a few gifts and envelopes. Josie took an envelope from her purse and added it to the others. A small Mariachi band played loud blaring music and some of the girls were dancing, their skirts twirling to the rhythm. A line was forming for the food and Maggie came up to them. "Thanks again for coming."

"Where are you planning on working?" Josie asked.

"I'm going back to the clinic as evening charge nurse." Maggie said proudly.

She seemed taller to Josie but maybe that was because she was thinner and her straight black hair was smartly cut just touching her shoulders. Josie scanned the room and wondered how Maggie would ever find a mate in this group that would live up to her potential.

"We have to go but I wish you the best. I know how lucky the clinic is to get you."

"Good luck to you." Paul added and they escaped before Maggie could insist they stay to eat. She blew them a kiss and turned back to her friends.

They were on the highway and. Josie put her hand on Paul's knee. "By the way where are we going?"

"We're going to a place called Sedona. Have you heard of it?"

"I don't think so."

"It's a beautiful place frequented by artists and tourists. The whole town is built on red rock and a river runs through it. There is a church sculptured out of rock high on the mountain that is exquisite. You'll love it."

As they wound their way through Oak Creek Canyon Josie was struck with the sheer beauty of the red rock changing hues from rose and mauve to the deepest rust. They pulled into a low one-story motel of pale pink stucco with a deep red tiled roof. It was nestled in rock only slightly darker and flowers of every shade grew in perfusion on either side of the tiled walkways.

Josie gasped, "Oh Paul what a beautiful spot."

The lobby was decorated in pastel from the bleached oak desk to the creamy leather couch and chairs. Pale peach and soft green pillows gave the air of peace and relaxation. The paintings were of flowering cactus, delicate humming birds and bowls of fruit.

"This décor is what the modern people call "southwest." Paul said. "No bright red and black Indian colors here."

"I have to admit I really do like the feeling of peace it gives you."

The next morning Paul and Josie wandered through the town, climbed the steep ascent to the chapel and shopped in Tepaki the walled area with small but exclusive shops. Arm and arm they explored, stopping to eat in an outdoor cafe and sometimes just pausing to gaze at the scenery and the rushing river as it wound its way over the rocks.

Two days later they began their journey toward the reservation. Turning off highway forty Josie noticed that they were nearly in New Mexico.

"I didn't realize the reservation was so near New Mexico."

"Yes," Paul said. "In fact Gallup is closer to the reservation than Flagstaff but it is still a small backward town."

Josie felt that for the first time she was really seeing not only the country but learning things about Paul as well.

They turned off the highway onto a narrower road that led to Window Rock but to Josie's surprise they kept going and finally pulled onto a gravel road that led to an impressive building where Paul came to a stop. "This is the new Navajo Community College. What do you think?"

"It's beautiful. The architecture is unusual."

"The large circular area is the library and modeled after the Navajo hogan. It's beautiful inside too. We will be open for students this fall."

"We?"

Paul grinned shyly. "You're looking at the new Dean."

Josie threw her arms around Paul "My darling, I am so proud of you."

Paul held her close to him and when he released her he cupped his hand under her chin and looked deep in her eyes. "Would you consider being the Dean's wife?"

Josie's eyes widened and she stared at Paul open mouthed and silent.

Paul broke the silence, "Jo, I'm sorry." He looked embarrassed and disappointed. "I didn't mean to blurt it out like that. I planned a romantic evening with candle light and music." His voice trailed off.

Josie circled her arms around his waist, "It was beautiful, I was just taken by surprise." She reached up and touched his cheek. "You know I love you Paul."

"But?"

"But," she held him tighter, "I have to think about the family, my home, my job. Will you please give me some time?"

Paul bent down and kissed her lips gently. "Of course I will. Come now I have one more thing to show you." He took her hand and pulled her back to the car.

Paul followed the gravel road and after a few miles turned into a winding drive that rose higher as they progressed. Suddenly a clearing came into view and they pulled into a driveway with a large garage and above it a house of golden cedar with a deck that circled as far as you could see. Tall windows rose to a peak and in the center a double wooden door.

Josie gasped "What a gorgeous house."

Paul jumped out of the car and went around to open Josie's door. He took her arm and they stood side by side gazing at the house. "It's mine," Paul said proudly, "or will be after thirty years of mortgage payments."

"All those years in your little cinderblock house and now this. I am just so proud of all you've accomplished."

"It's really close to the college. The only problem is that it's quite a way from grocery stores. The man who built it wanted privacy and when he died suddenly his wife wanted to be closer to civilization and her children."

Paul pushed a button on his key chain and the garage door opened. "Let's go in this way." The steps led to a laundry room which in turn led to the kitchen. It was modern with gleaming appliances, tile counters and a cozy breakfast bar with two stools. There was also a built in desk on which sat Paul's computer. Apparently he had already been living here although he had not mentioned it.

The living room was what was called a great room since it contained a round table with four chairs, couches and chairs of burnished leather with colorful pillows. The floors were wood with large colorful rugs that were the same shades as the pillows. A fireplace of natural rock rose between the windows and the mantel was made of the same polished wood that trimmed the windows.

"It's all so beautiful, I don't know what to say." Josie ran her hand over the soft leather couch."

"It was already furnished and everything came with the house. Mrs. Henley took only personal items. Said she wanted something more feminine."

Josie laughed. "He must have been the boss."

Paul led the way into the bedroom that was furnished with wood and earthy colors. The bed was large and flanked by tables and lamps and Josie noticed a stack of books on the nightstand next to one side.

"There is one other bedroom but it's quite small and has only a small trundle bed. So what do you think?" Paul said anxiously.

"I think you got a really good deal." Josie looked up at him and smiled. "I think I could get to like it here."

Paul was happy that Josie was impressed and even if she was teasing him about liking it she must at least be thinking about his proposal. She was the only person he could imagine being with for the rest of his life. He thought of Nick and how he had escaped injury in the war only to die of cancer years later. Still he knew that he and Josie had many years left to enjoy life and each other. He also wondered how he measured up to Nick in ways that would make her happy. He knew that Nick was a party person, loved to entertain, and of course that was out of Paul's realm. And there were the family dinners. Would she miss being near her children every day? Paul hoped he had not frightened her off by rushing his proposal.

Paul took Josie for a walk around the property. It was such a beautiful spot. The trees were dense pines and squirrels darted among the fragrant branches and chattered at the intruders. In the distance sun glistened on the narrow fingers of snow that lingered on the mountains. Tiny sprouts of wild flowers peeked from their winter covering of pine needles. Josie dropped to her knees to smell the wild purple violets. "Everything is so fresh and new."

Paul pulled her to her feet and circled her in his arms. "I feel that way about myself, my life. It will be new and fresh and filled with promise."

Arm and arm they returned to the house. Paul went to the freezer and took out two small steaks. "I think I can put together a pretty decent meal. I don't have anything for salad but I have frozen vegetables and we can bake a couple potatoes."

"Sounds wonderful." Josie picked up a book and snuggled down in the leather chair. Music was playing softly and a fire crackled and hissed as the sap oozed from the logs.

It's too good to be true you know. Whenever things are too perfect something bad always happens .I was on the verge of becoming rich and successful until they destroyed me. J.J. would have been a great writer and instead look what happened .Be careful you don't spoil Paul's career. Nick's voice was familiar and yet far away. How dare he make it sound like being happy was a sin.

"Jo, wake up. You poor darling. I must have worn you out. You've been asleep over an hour." Paul smoothed her hair back from her eyes and kissed her forehead.

She pulled him to her and kissed him fiercely. She clung to him and kissed him again and again. He unbuttoned her blouse and cradled her breast. His head dropped to take it in his mouth and she was straining toward him moaning. He lifted her in his arms and took her to the bed.

Later as they lay wrapped in each other's arms and happily exhausted. Josie thought how much she enjoyed Paul and everything they did. Would it last the rest of their life? Paul slid out of bed and leaned over and kissed her gently. "I'd better get started on that dinner I promised you."

The shadows had deepened into twilight and Josie could see the stars beginning to appear. The French doors that opened onto the wraparound deck would be the perfect place to sit on a warm summer's night. Josie rose and opened the suitcase Paul had brought to the room. She extracted a warm sweat shirt with matching pants and pulling them on and went into the kitchen. Paul was scrubbing two large potatoes at the sink. She encircled his waist. "Can I help?"

He turned his head to kiss her. "You *may* set the table. The dishes are in that cupboard." He nodded toward it. The patio door was open and charcoal glowed deep red in the grill.

When dinner was over they took their wine to the sofa in front of the fireplace.

"That was a great dinner!" Josie held up her glass. "A toast to the chef."

Their glasses clinked and they leaned back to sip the garnet liquid.

Paul set his glass down and took a small velvet box from his pocket. "Josephine, will you wear this ring while you think about my proposal?" He took from the box a turquoise ring set in silver surrounded by diamonds and taking her hand in his, slipped it on her finger.

"Paul, it's exquisite. I do love you very much and I promise I'll give you my answer very soon." She put her arms around him and kissed him deeply. "I want to be here with you forever but I also want to talk to the children, ok?"

"Sure, now I want to show you some things about the college." His voice was enthusiastic and he showed her pictures of the finished college. They talked for a long time and the ring sparkled on Josie's finger.

The next few days flew by and it was time for Josie to return to Colorado. The last evening Paul prepared the house for leaving as he planned to drive Josie home, stay the night and then return.

"I'm going to miss you so much. I can't imagine being here without you." Paul was on his knees cleaning the fireplace and looked up at her with a forlorn expression in his dark eyes. "Is there any chance you'll come back for the summer?"

"I'm sorry Paul, but I do have a job. I promise we'll work something out."

Paul went to wash his hands and when he came back he took Josie in his arms and whispered, "Please think about marrying me. I need you to fill this house with joy."

The following morning Paul and Josie set off for Colorado. Spring was in full bloom and wild flowers of purple and yellow ran amok through the fields. Trees were sprouting their green leaves and the sun shone bright and warmed the inside of the car. Paul was very quiet and Josie talked lightly of the past week and how happy she was. She looked at Paul for confirmation but his countenance was almost sullen. Josie decided he might be pouting because she had not responded more to his proposal but then she noticed that he seemed to grimace with pain.

"Is something wrong?"

Paul shook his head but was gripping the steering wheel so hard his knuckles had turned white. Josie had never given much thought to Paul's useless arm since he seemed to be able to do anything necessary with his right but now she noticed that he was having a hard time driving with only one arm.

"Paul pull over here at this turnoff."

Paul turned the car and stopped. "Something is wrong. My left arm is throbbing and I haven't felt anything in it for years."

Josie leaned over and touched his forehead. "My God you're burning up!"

Paul grasped his left arm and a spasm of pain went through his body. "I don't understand this."

"Move over and I'll drive. We've got to get you to a doctor."

They exchanged places and Josie drove. They were already in Colorado but a long way from Denver. They were just coming down a steep incline that led into the city of Grand Junction. Josie pulled into the first service station she saw. She ran inside and asked the girl behind the counter, "Could you tell me where the nearest emergency room is?"

"About two blocks, turn left and you'll see the hospital from there."

"Thanks." Josie ran back to the car. "How is it?"

" I'll be ok let's just keep going."

"Paul let me take you to a doctor and let him have a look."
Paul was in no position to argue so he leaned back and closed
his eyes.

Josie parked the car in the emergency room entrance and ran
inside.

"Please I need help. My friend is very ill." Quickly an
attendant brought a wheel chair and guided Paul into it and
rushed him inside. Josie tried to follow but the clerk stopped
her.

"You'll need to fill out some paperwork." The clerk said in
a business-like tone and handed Josie a clipboard.

"I'll need his wallet," Josie said. "May I go in and get it?"
She nodded toward the double doors.

The clerk sighed, "I guess so but you have to come right
back ok?"

Josie nodded and pushed open the door. She saw Paul in one
of the cubicles and his pants lay on the chair. A lab person in a
white coat was drawing blood and the doctor was making notes
on the chart.

"Excuse me; I need to get his wallet." Josie said.

"How long has your husband had this fever?" The doctor
asked.

Josie ignored the word husband. " It began some time in the
night but we were heading for Denver and he thought it would
subside. He took some aspirin and seemed better so we kept
going but it got worse."

"He appears to have a serious infection. Does he have any
allergies? I would like to start an IV antibiotic right away."

"I uh, I really don't know for sure. He's not my husband,
just a friend."

The doctor's eyebrow raised slightly and he bent over Paul.
"Do you have any allergies?"

Paul shook his head and the doctor turned back to Josie. "I'm going to start the IV and I'll come and talk to you when the blood work comes back. I should know more by then."

Dismissed, Josie went back to the desk and filled out the papers the best she could and sat down in the waiting room.

Josie leaned back and closed her eyes. Another waiting room, another decision she thought except that this time it was not her husband or son and she really had no business making decisions for Paul. She prayed that he would be all right. She looked up as she heard the doctor, "Mrs Begay?"

"No, I told you Mr. Begay is a friend."

"Yes, of course. I'm sorry to tell you this but after the tests and x-rays I have concluded that he will probably have to have that arm amputated."

"My God, what is it?"

"There is a tumor blocking the blood supply to the arm and it has been that way for a while and now the arm is deteriorating of gangrene. If the tumor is malignant it could spread."

"Have you discussed this with him?"

"I did but he has had considerable pain medication and I'm not sure he fully understood."

"May I see him?"

"Yes, of course."

Josie followed the doctor into a cubicle where Paul lay on a narrow cot. The doctor left the room and Josie sat on the straight chair beside the bed. She leaned over and kissed his cheek. "Paul?"

"A fine mess isn't it?"

Josie swallowed her tears. "If you have to have surgery I would like to get you to Denver. I know the doctors there and they have everything at their disposal. Would you agree?"

Paul nodded, "Do whatever you think is best. I'm so sorry to cause you all this trouble."

Josie laid her cheek against his. "Please don't feel like that. I love you Paul and I'll make arrangements to transfer you, ok?"

When Josie told the doctor she wanted Paul transferred to Denver he agreed as long as he went by ambulance or helicopter so they could keep the IV running. Josie called Danny, told him, and then called the orthopedic doctor and soon arrangements were made. Paul would go by helicopter and Josie would drive the car and meet them there.

"Have a nice trip." Josie kissed Paul gently as they wheeled him to the helipad and she headed for the car. It would be much longer for her but it would give her time to think.

Chapter XXIII
Colorado

When Josie arrived in Denver she went straight to the hospital. She could call Danny from there. Mary Beth would have to be called too although she was expecting them to stay at the house. It would be different now. Josie wondered if Paul had given any thought as to who would be responsible if he was unable to make decisions about the hospital or his finances. Josie went to the desk and asked for Paul Begay's room number. The girl behind the desk looked at a list wrinkled her forehead and then got up to talk to a nurse who was charting. After a brief conversation she came back.

"Are you his wife?" The clerk asked.

"No, but..."

Quickly she interrupted.

"We're not allowed to give information except to family."

Josie tried to be patient. "I know, but he has no family here."

Again the clerk went to talk to the nurse. The nurse rose and came to the desk. "Now what's the problem?"

Josie explained the situation and added, "Actually I'm his fiancée' and I work at this hospital on third floor."

"I thought I recognized you." The nurse was smiling now. "You're Mrs. Romano and you have a son who's a doctor too. Your fiancée is in surgery."

"Thank you so much."

"You may wait in the surgery waiting room if you wish."

"Thanks." Josie hurried to the waiting room. They sure didn't lose any time getting him into surgery she thought.

"Mom." Danny touched his mother gently.

Josie was startled and came awake still groggy. "What is it?"

"It's okay. Paul is in the recovery room and the doctor would like to talk to you."

"Okay."

Danny led her to a small office where the doctor was dictating. He laid aside the microphone and turned off the machine. "The surgery went well and Mr. Begay will be taken to his room soon where you may see him."

"Thank you. He has no family here so I appreciate your giving me the information."

The doctor smiled and nodded toward Danny. "Dr. Romano has explained. I want to set up rehab as soon as possible. They fit the patients with a prosthesis when the stitches heal and he should get started as soon as possible. As for the malignancy I sent some samples to the lab but I think we got it all. I want to see him in my office in a week"

Josie nodded. "His home is in a rural area of Arizona so I'm going to suggest to him that he stay in Denver until he feels capable of returning home."

"Good enough." The doctor shook hands with each of them and returned to his dictation.

Josie squeezed Danny's arm. "Thanks for coming with me."

"Sure. Do you really think Paul will stay here that long?"

"I think so. You know Paul was appointed Dean of the new Indian College and this is going to be a blow to him. He'll need lots of encouragement. Also he asked me to marry him."

Danny laughed, "We all guessed as much. We talk about you behind your back, you know."

Josie punched his arm. "Honestly I wasn't sure myself."

"Do you think you'll be happy living there?"

"Yes I do but I was worried about leaving all of you."

"Mom we're all settled and not that far away. We'll be fine."

"Right now I want to stay until Paul comes out of recovery and is settled in his room. I'll call Mary Beth and tell her what's going on."

"I called both Mary Beth and David and told them he was going to surgery."

"Thanks. What would I do without you?"

Danny grinned. He liked being able to help her.

Josie waited until the nurse came to inform her that Paul was in his room.

"I imagine he'll sleep most of the day but I thought you'd want to see him for a few minutes at least."

"Yes, thanks. I won't stay long."

Paul lay pale and still against the white sheets. A feeling of deep tenderness came over Josie as she stood over him. She bent and kissed him lightly. He opened his eyes and smiled weakly. "So it's over?"

"Yes, the doctor said you did fine. They're sending the surrounding tissue to test for cancer cells but he thinks they got it all."

"Good."

"I'll let you sleep now but I'll be back first thing in the morning."

"Thanks for everything." His breath caught in his throat and the moisture in his eyes was unusual for Paul. Josie kissed him again and left the room.

That evening Josie and Mary Beth sat at the kitchen table enjoying a cup of tea. The baby was in bed and Peter was in the den doing paper work. Josie had asked Mary Beth if she would mind if Paul came here and they stayed until he had finished rehab. "Of course you can stay here. It is still your house."

"Not really. You and Peter are paying the mortgage and I am hoping you may want to buy it. Paul and I are planning on getting married and I'll move to Arizona."

"Really Mother, are you sure you want to live around Indians the rest of your life?" Her voice had a definite edge.

Josie shook her head and looked at her daughter in surprise. "After all Paul *is* Indian and I have spent a lot of time there. I thought you liked Paul."

"I do, but when I think of you *living* there forever I...." she stopped and shrugged her shoulders. "Why can't he move here?"

"He has been appointed Dean of the new Indian College." Josie said proudly.

"All the worse. You won't see anyone but Indians and those awful houses they live in."

Josie was quite taken back by Mary Beth's attitude and yet, she thought, I was thinking the same thing not too long ago. She sighed and decided to leave it for tonight. She was bushed and certainly didn't want to argue with her daughter.

The next morning Josie felt refreshed and flinging open the bedroom window she drew a deep breath. A flowering plum tree bursting with delicate lavender blossoms was so close she could almost touch it. The heavy scent filled her nostrils and lifted her spirits. She grabbed her robe and ran downstairs.

Mary Beth was feeding Annie her cereal and there was as much outside as in. Annie squealed in delight at seeing her grandmother and Josie bent to kiss the curly headed little girl who looked so much like her mother had at that age.

"Good morning." Mary Beth rose to pour the coffee.

"Good morning dear, sit still. I'll get the coffee."

They sat sipping their coffee and Josie broke the silence. "I thought I'd ask Paul to come here for a few days when he's released. Is that all right with you?"

"Of course mother. I'm sorry if I spoke out of turn last night."

"It's all right darling. You're entitled to your opinion."

Mary Beth looked miserable. "I didn't mean anything against Paul."

"I know, we'll discuss it at a later date, ok?"

When Josie arrived at Paul's room he was sitting in a chair and had already had his breakfast and a bath. She crossed the room and kissed him and pulled up the only other chair beside him. "How are you feeling?"

"Not bad at all. It feels strange as though it's still there."

Josie nodded. "I know that's what they all say. Have you talked to the doctor?""

"Yes, he was here really early. He says I can go home tomorrow and start therapy Monday morning."

"That's great. The sooner the better."

"Jo, I've been thinking and I'm not sure I want to keep my commitment as Dean."

"Paul, How can you say that? You said it was a dream come true."

"That was before. I'm not sure I can handle having a plastic arm and I sure can't go around with a safety pin holding up my empty sleeve."

Josie leaned over and took Paul's face in her hands. "Listen to me my darling. The new prosthetics they have now are wonderful. You can pick up a pencil or even a paper clip. They're lightweight and if you really want to look fancy you can get one with a hand that looks absolutely real." Josie paused and looked deep into the brown depths of his eyes. She kissed his lips. "I love you Paul and I want very much to be a Dean's wife."

Paul closed his eyes and tears rolled slowly down his cheeks. He put his good arm around Josie and held her close. "If you're with me I'll try my best."

The day Paul was discharged Josie brought him home and established him in the master bedroom where she and Nick had spent so many years. It was evident that Mary Beth did not wholly approve of her mother sleeping with Paul without benefit of marriage. She was a staunch member of the Catholic community and this would not set well with the parishioners who had known the family for many years. Josie felt it was her own business and who would actually know if she was sleeping with him or if he was just a guest. Still this did put a strain on her relationship with Mary Beth for the first time in their life.

The rehab hospital was one of the largest and most prestigious in the country. Many famous athletes who were injured came here and soldiers from the war in Viet Nam were sent here when the Government hospitals became over-crowded. Seeing the young boys missing legs and arms was difficult for Paul. Viet Nam had seemed far away from Arizona and Paul could not believe that already another conflict was destroying the young men of still another generation.

"I always believed that "our" war would be the last one but it is never so." Paul's voice was husky; his eyes filled with despair and the loss of his arm seemed inconsequential compared to what he saw among others.

"Keep in mind all the good you'll be doing with the education of the young men of your race."

"I hope so. Why can't there be peace among people of every race?" Paul looked at the woman he loved with her honey colored hair now tinged with gray and her skin so fair and a wave of jubilation coursed through his veins that this precious white woman had given him her heart.

Paul sat exercising his arm with the prosthesis attached as his therapist had instructed him. His eyes were drawn to the patient on the parallel bars. He was young and his features were obviously Indian. There was no mistaking the high cheekbones and full lips. His dark eyes were filled with pain as he tried valiantly to walk on two artificial legs. His mouth was set in a straight line and there was bitterness in the fine lines that seemed to belie his youth. Paul's heart went out to him and he was ashamed of his own feelings about losing an arm that had been useless for decades. What an ass I am he admonished himself.

"How are you doing?" It was Liz his therapist. "I've been watching you and you seem to have lost your concentration."

"Sorry, I was wondering about that guy over on the bars. He seems so young."

"Yes he is. He had barely turned eighteen when he was sent to Viet Nam and now here he is already a veteran." She shook her head sadly.

"Where's he from?"

"Some Indian reservation in New Mexico."

"I'd like to meet him."

Liz winked at him. "I think I can arrange that."

A short time later Liz wheeled the exhausted young man next to Paul as she went to get them both a glass of juice. "Good workout" she called over her shoulder. The young man wiped his face.

"My name's Paul Begay." Paul said with a nod.

"Joe Toledo. You Indian?"

"Navajo. I served in WWII."

"Yeah, my father too. We're Zuni but I've met a lot of Navajo."

By the time they had finished their juice and Tom, the orderly, came to take Joe back to his room they had become friends.

Liz was delighted. "You're the first person I've seen Joe talk to." She said. "It's been a real rough time for him."

"I'm glad. I enjoyed it too."

When Josie came to pick up Paul he told her about Joe. "Just think if I could get him to come up to the school."

"So the school's looking pretty good again." She teased.

"Yeah, you were right. They need me and I need them. It's going to be a great year."

The remaining days of Paul's therapy he saw Joe Toledo every day and they became more than just patients but the best of friends. Paul had been a mentor to several boys during his years of teaching but never had he been as close to any of them as he was to Joe. They had both been brought up on a reservation. Both of them had fathers killed in World War II and were brought up by single mothers. Paul had always known that he wanted an education and had worked and saved and pursued grants to realize his dream of being a teacher. Joe had dropped out of school on the reservation and hung out with the gangs who still used *peyote* the drug made from cacti that did strange things to their minds and the action that followed. The beer that they were forbidden to drink was smuggled into the reservation and was very plentiful. Once Joe had wanted to do something with his life but the desire had fled in a hazy cloud of *peyote*. He had thought the army would give him a new chance and then this had happened. A young girl had come up to him from a village where they had taken out a nest of enemy soldiers. She looked so forlorn as she held out her hand begging for food that Joe felt a wave of guilt for the destruction of their village. Joe had a small piece of chocolate in his breast pocket and reached in to give it to her. Just then she had thrown a grenade toward the ground and Joe had crumpled in pain, the chocolate still in his hand. When he woke up in the hospital he knew that both of his legs were gone and devastation washed over him. It was the end of his dreams for a better life and his bitterness for a war that he did not understand had once again eroded the desire to try to make a new start.

Paul had given some of that desire back to him. He admired the soft spoken professor who had told him about the new college soon to open and the lines around his mouth seemed to soften when he told his therapist that just possibly he could qualify to study there. Liz was thankful to Paul for giving this patient hope for his future.

"Congratulations." Dr.Scott said with a grin. "You've been approved by the therapist to be discharged from our services."

Paul and Josie hugged each other and shook hands with the doctor. Paul asked Josie to come and meet the young man he had told her about and they went to find him. Joe was working the parallel bars as usual. Sometimes Liz had to make him stop he was so determined to master the task of walking.

"Joe, I just got my walking papers from the Doc and I wanted to say good-by."

Joe grinned. "Thanks for everything. I'm really going to look you up when I get out. I'm going to get my GED and then try to get into your school."

"Good for you. I'd like you to meet Josephine."

Josie reached out to take his hand and when he tried to take his hand off the bar he faltered. "Sorry, I'm glad to meet you."

"Joe, I want you to know we'd be happy to have you come and visit us."

"Thank you."

Paul put his arm lightly around Joe's shoulder. "We'll keep in touch. I'll write to you and send you some information. "So long, friend."

"Good-by. I'll write." His voice choked and tears glazed his eyes.

Paul took Josie's arm and hurried out the door.

After all this time they would finally be able to go back to Arizona and Paul's home in the mountains.

Chapter XXIV
Arizona
1968

The scenery was changing now as Paul and Josie climbed higher. Pine trees grew tall and thick and colorful wild flowers wound their way among the trunks and converged near a clear stream that rushed and curled from the runoff above. Josie rolled down the window and the scent of pine filled the car.

"Oh Paul, it's so beautiful and the air so pure. I'm happy we'll be living up here." Just then a small clearing came into view filled with orange poppies waving and bobbing in the breeze. "Let's stop here for a few minutes." Josie clasped her hands "These poppies are gorgeous."

Paul stopped the car at the side of the road and smiled. "I'm sure some enterprising young Navajo is harvesting them for opium."

"Oh no, you'll spoil it for me."

They laughed together and Paul pulled back into the road. In a short time they were pulling into Paul's driveway.

They had packed a small U-Haul trailer with Josie's personal things. A few books and small pieces of furniture and knick-knacks that would make it feel like home.

A week later Josie was puttering with some pots she had filled with flowers and felt she had lived here forever. Paul came down the path waving a letter. "The first meeting of the faculty and board is in two weeks."

"Wonderful." Josie looked at Paul's happy face. "What would you think about having a little party here after the meeting so everyone could get acquainted?"

"Are you sure you want to go to that much trouble?"

"I'd love to do it."

"You're going to make a great Dean's wife." Paul pulled her into his arms and brushed his lips across her nose then found her mouth and kissed her deeply.

"Speaking of your wife, what would you think about making it official and saying our vows at that little chapel in the woods just outside the village?"

Paul swallowed the lump that rose in his throat. "It would make me the happiest man on earth." He kissed her again but this time he picked her up in his arms and carried her into the bedroom.

They were married the following Saturday by the young priest who came weekly to hear confessions. They bribed him to stay and marry them by offering him a steak dinner with wine and all the trimmings prepared by the groom. He was happy to do so and beamed at the handsome Navajo and the pretty blond woman in her soft chiffon dress carrying a bouquet of wild flowers.

The priest followed them home and shared their table and blessed the food and the marriage and left feeling a warm glow that did not come often enough in his young ministry.

As for Paul and Josie they went to bed as always, their hands with the matching silver bands held tight and their love making passionate.

"I love you Mrs. BeGay." Paul's voice was husky "I feel as though my life is just beginning."

"I know." Josie let her fingers trail down his face. "This is a new beginning for us both and I know it will last forever." The kiss they shared this time led to new heights for them both and when at last they lay exhausted, sleep came peacefully and bathed them in moonglow.

EPILOGUE
Arizona 2003

The invitation came in the morning mail. It looked expensive and had the official seal of the president of the United States. Paul opened it gingerly and glanced at the contents. He turned to Josie who had come into the room and handed it to her.

"What do you make of this?"

She read it slowly. "It seems that the President wishes to present you with a medal to recognize you for your heroic service in the army."

Paul raised his eyebrows and with a quizzical grin he muttered, "Good God, that was over fifty years ago."

"Then it's about time." Josie said, smiling up at him.

November 14, 2003
Washington DC

The distinguished couple, their similar trench coats with rust colored scarves wound under their chins against the cold November wind, walked down the aisle looking from side to side for their seats. Both had hair as white as the clouds that sailed across the sky but they walked straight and tall. As the seats began to fill they spotted those assigned to them and sat close, their hands clasped.

The reporter covering the event knew that most of the Indian population lived in New Mexico, Arizona, and other southwestern states where this time of year it was still warm so it was perhaps not the best of days to have a ceremony out of doors.

The occasion was National American Indian Heritage Month and President George W. Bush had invited American Indians and those of Alaska to come to the signing of the Proclamation. The fact that once again native Americans were serving in the armed forces in the unpopular war in Iraq was probably part of the reason for this timely observance.

The United States Marine Corp band played as the President approached the podium. He opened with a welcome and then in his best political voice, he went on to praise the many American Indians and Alaska Natives who are serving on active duty in Iraq. Lowering his voice in a deeply sincere tone he went on. "Lori Piestewa, a member of the Hopi tribe and a Specialist of the Army's 507th Maintenance Company was the first American woman killed in Operation Iraqi Freedom and the only known American Indian woman killed in action in any conflict. Her bravery, service, and sacrifice are an inspiration to our men and women in uniform and to all Americans."

The sun finally came from behind a cloud and shone brilliantly on the Capital. Dome. It was an awe-inspiring sight. The military band stood at attention and red white and blue bunting decorated the stage.

The President, looking young and fit, extolled the roll of the American Indian as he continued. "My administration has proposed in the 2004 budget to spend over $11 billion on Native American programs." Polite applause interrupted him.

He went on to say the Department of Education's office of American Indian Education would have access to nearly $122 million in grants to improve education opportunities. In addition, a program would include $49 million for tribal colleges and universities. He added that they were also working to address the healthcare needs of American Indians. He concluded that portion of his speech and the audience applauded.

Acknowledging the applause, the President waved and smiled and then in a strong voice proclaimed,

" NOW, THEREFORE, I, GEORGE W BUSH, President of the United States of America, by virtue of the authority vested in me by the Constitution and laws of the United States, do hereby proclaim November, 2003 National American Indian Heritage Month. IN WITNESS WHEREOF, I have hereunto set my hand this fourteenth day of November in the year of our Lord two thousand three, and of the Independence of the United States of America the two hundred and twenty-eighth."

The proclamation signed, the President stood and with the band playing left the podium.

The General and head of the Armed Forces then began to read off names and hand out medals that had been long forgotten, as well as those from the present conflict.

The reporter was leaving to file his story when the name Paul M Begay was called and the distinguished looking man in the trench coat walked tall and straight to receive it. It was the Medal of Honor from World War II and was given for military heroism above and beyond the call of duty. Paul was cited for saving the life of a fellow soldier and wiping out a nest of Japanese soldiers. Also saving an unknown number of American soldiers on Iwo Jima by reporting in Navajo code the day and time of a heavy artillery attack.

The reporter, covering the ceremony shook his head. Receiving the Medal of Honor fifty-eight years late. He wondered how many had gone to their graves without recognition.

Josie watched as the General handed Paul the medal. She saw him take it with his prosthetic hand and then give a smart salute. She smiled as he came back toward her and sat down. He handed her the medal and she saw the moisture in his eyes. She knew it was not the medal that caused the tears but the memories it brought with it. His memories of Nick and Sam Running Horse and James would be clear in his mind. Who would have ever thought that she and Paul would come together and be married for all these years. Thank God her children had adjusted to the marriage and they were close enough to Colorado that they saw the children and the grandchildren often.

Paul had been so happy as the Dean of the Navajo Community College. Later the name had been changed to Dine College [college of the people.] In 1976 it had been accredited and in 1998 they had bestowed Bachelor Degrees under the Dine teacher education program in partnership with Arizona State University.

Paul had mentored so many young people over the years including the young man from New Mexico that he met at the Rehab Hospital. Joe Toledo had gone on to the University and become a successful architect and designed many buildings in the New Mexico area.

After Paul retired, Joe and many of his other students kept in contact with him and invited him to speak at seminars and participate in reunions and other events. Josie was proud to be the wife of such a man. No matter what had been done to the Indian Nation in former years Paul had always been a true American and had said many times that America would always be the Home of the Brave and the Land of the Free.

Paul leaned toward her. "Can we get out of here now?"

Slipping the medal into her purse Josie took Paul's hand and together they slipped away.

At the hotel Paul guided Josie to a booth in the bar that was nearly deserted in the afternoon. "We should have a glass of wine to celebrate this magnificent occasion." His grin made him look almost young and very endearing.

"You forget, we hardly drink any more."

"That's okay we don't have to drive so we can just have a glass of wine and go upstairs and take a nap."

Josie laughed. " A nap or a roll in the hay?"

"My, my, what a suspicious mind you have, Mrs Begay."

They slid into the soft leather booth and ordered. Paul was pensive.

"You know that was a bunch of bull. All that stuff the President said. We'll never get all those grants. Politics that's all it is. That and guilt the Indian girl got killed in this fool war."

"You darling man I love you so, but we've done all we can do I think. Let's just go home and enjoy what's left of our life."

The waiter set the wine down and they each picked up their glass. Paul swirled the garnet liquid and lifted his glass. "To the most wonderful wife in the world. Without you I would have never lived and loved."

Josie's blue eyes sparkled as she lifted her glass. "To my handsome romantic husband who knows that we will never grow old in our hearts."

Their eyes met and as their glasses clinked and even as they drank they were looking forward to that nap and being together in the warmth and ecstasy of their enduring love.

Acknowledgements

The Book of the Navajo by Raymond Friday Locke
Navajo Code Talkers by Nathan Aaseng
The Pacific War by consultant editor Bernard C. Nalty
Century by Peter Jennings and Todd Brewster
Southwest Studies, a course by Harry Swanson, Ph.D who stirred up my interest in the American Indian.
American Indians-Presidential Proclamation 2003/Americans.net

Todd Engel cover art

Will Carnahan, my friend and colleague who edited my efforts.

My thanks to all.

Printed in the United Kingdom
by Lightning Source UK Ltd.
128144UK00001B/406/P